‘You don’t want a wife?’

‘If I opted for a marriage of convenience instead, the problem would vanish. That kind of marriage might last between five and ten years max, before ending in an amicable divorce.’

‘Why are you telling me this?’

‘I think there’s a possibility that we could reach a mutually beneficial agreement,’ Antonio murmured thoughtfully. ‘The wife I choose would have to know the score. I would expect to retain my freedom to come and go as and when I liked, and with whom I pleased.’

‘You’re talking about a fake marriage?’ Sophie pressed uncertainly. ‘Are you suggesting that you and *me*—?’

‘You’d be insane to turn me down.’

Lynne Graham was born in Northern Ireland and has been a keen Mills & Boon® reader since her teens. She is very happily married, with an understanding husband who has learned to cook since she started to write! Her five children keep her on her toes. She has a very large dog, which knocks everything over, a very small terrier, which barks a lot, and two cats. When time allows, she is a keen gardener. Lynne published her fiftieth Mills and Boon® title in 2004.

Recent titles by the same author:

THE GREEK TYCOON'S CONVENIENT MISTRESS
THE MISTRESS WIFE

MARRIED BY ARRANGEMENT

BY

LYNNE GRAHAM

First published in Great Britain 2005
Harlequin Mills & Boon Limited,
Eton House, 18-24 Paradise Road, Richmond, Surrey TW9 1SR

ISBN 0 263 84151 0

Set in Times Roman 10½ on 12 pt.
01-0605-49723

Printed and bound in Spain
by Litografia Rosés, S.A., Barcelona

CHAPTER ONE

'BUT why didn't Belinda tell us last year that she had given birth to Pablo's child?' Antonio Rocha, Marqués de Salazar, demanded of his grandmother, lingering astonishment etched in the hard set of his sculpted cheekbones, his lean, darkly handsome face grim.

'We barely got to know Belinda while your brother was alive.' Doña Ernesta's fine-boned features reflected her regret over that state of affairs. 'How could we expect her to turn to us for help after he had abandoned her?'

'I tried several times to set up a meeting with Belinda. She always made excuses,' Antonio reminded the older woman. 'Finally, she insisted that she didn't need our help and she made it clear that she no longer regarded us as being related to her.'

'Her pride may have spoken for her. I imagine Pablo left her with little else. Now that we know that he must have deserted her when she was pregnant, my heart is even heavier,' Doña Ernesta confessed. 'Yet when he married her, I truly believed that he might finally settle down.'

Being an incurable cynic, Antonio had had no such hopes. After all, his younger brother had broken the heart of his own family long before he had graduated to wreaking havoc beyond that select circle. Although born with every advantage into the most élite stratum of Spanish high society, Pablo had started getting in trouble at an early age.

His parents had found it impossible to control him. By the time Pablo had reached his early twenties, he had dissipated a substantial inheritance and defrauded several relatives and friends of large amounts of money. Throughout those troubled years, countless people had made repeated efforts to understand, correct and solve Pablo's problems. All such attempts had been unsuccessful, not least, Antonio believed, because his brother had got a huge kick out of breaking the law and swindling the foolish.

It was three years since Pablo had come home to mend fences and announce his intention of marrying his beautiful English girlfriend. Overjoyed by his return, Doña Ernesta had insisted on throwing the wedding for the happy couple while at the same time making them a very generous gift of money. The marriage, however, had failed and Pablo had returned to Spain twelve months ago. Soon afterwards, the younger man had lost his life in a drunken car crash.

'It astonishes me that Pablo could have kept such a secret from us,' Doña Ernesta lamented. 'It is even more sad that Belinda could not trust us enough to share her child with us.'

'I've made arrangements to fly over to London tomorrow morning,' Antonio told her, frowning when the elderly woman seated by the elegant marble fireplace continued to look deeply troubled. 'Try not to dwell on your sorrow. As a family, we did all that we could and we will now do our very best for Pablo's daughter.'

It was only that afternoon that Antonio had received an urgent call from the family lawyer, who had in turn been contacted by Belinda's solicitor in England. Antonio had been sincerely shaken by the news that his brother's widow had not only given birth to a child six months earlier, but had died from pneumonia just a fortnight ago. He had been relieved that, independent though Belinda had evidently intended to be, she had still had the foresight and sense to nominate him in her will as the guardian of her daughter, Lydia. At the family lawyer's instigation, however, Antonio had also agreed that, even though he had no reason to doubt that the little girl was his brother's child, DNA testing, distasteful though it was, would be a sensible precaution.

The lawyer had then informed him that Belinda's sister, Sophie, was currently looking after the child. Dismayed by that information, Antonio had appreciated that his own intervention was immediately required. Sophie was far too young for such a responsibility and he thought it unlikely that her lifestyle would be conducive to the care of a baby.

Antonio had met Sophie when she had acted as a bridesmaid at her sister's wedding. The pronounced differences between the two sisters had disconcerted his conservative family. While Belinda had had the confident gloss and clear diction of the British middle class, Sophie had appeared to hail from a rather less privileged background. Indeed Antonio's English had been much more grammatically correct than hers had been. As he recalled those unexplained discrepancies his incisive gaze veiled. An involuntary memory of Sophie with her tumbling fall of blonde curls and glinting green eyes assailed Antonio. Not a beauty in the classic elegant style of her sister, certainly. Even so, Antonio had found his attention continually returning to the youngest, smallest bridesmaid that day and he had been equally quick to notice that there wasn't a man in the room impervious to her appeal.

But her apparent appeal had been very short-lived,

Antonio reminded himself grimly, his expressive mouth curling with disdain. Sophie had been sparkling, sexy and intensely feminine. But as he had discovered she had also been a slut. Watching her trail back into her hotel at dawn with her youthful lover and with her clothing dishevelled from a night of passion on the beach had been a salutary lesson. Clearly, she had been no more particular in her habits than the many tourists who came to Spain to indulge in rampant casual sex and an excess of alcohol.

'A little girl. My first great-grandchild,' Doña Ernesta remarked with a tentative smile softening her rather severe features, her well-modulated speaking voice breaking into what was a rare moment of abstraction for her grandson. 'Lydia. It is a pretty name. A baby will transform the *castillo*.'

Antonio resisted a dismayingly strong urge to wince while inwardly acknowledging that he had been in no great hurry to embrace fatherhood. He was barely thirty years old. He had yet to experience the faintest glimmer of a desire to produce the next generation and had never had the slightest interest in babies. In fact he generally gave the rug rats a fairly wide berth at family events. Doubtless the perceived charm of a howling baby lay in the fond eye of its parent and magically enabled the parent to overlook the fact that babies were horrifically noisy and messy.

'I imagine so,' Antonio murmured wryly, resolving to have the nursery suite in the little-used east wing renovated at speed. He would also ensure that a full complement of staff was hired to service the child's every need.

He was not ashamed to admit that he liked his life just as it was. He had had to work incredibly hard for a very long time to repair the damage done to the Rocha family fortunes by Pablo's ceaseless depredations. While his brother had been running wild and free on his ill-gotten gains, Antonio had been working eighteen-hour days. Self-indulgence, personal interests and relaxation had all been luxuries out of Antonio's reach. Having since amassed sufficient wealth to be judged a billionaire, Antonio now relished his own highly sophisticated existence, his fantastic social life and his freedom to do exactly as he liked.

But he was equally well aware that change was in the air: Pablo's daughter was now his personal responsibility. It was his duty to take charge of the orphaned infant and bring her back to Spain. It was right and fitting that this should be the case, Antonio conceded. The baby was of his blood and part of his family and he would raise her as though she were his own daughter.

'You'll have to get married, of course,' his grandmother murmured in a voice as soft and light as thistledown.

Startled by that disconcerting assurance, Antonio swung back to survey the old lady, who was carefully addressing her attention to her needlework. Grudging amusement glinted in his clear dark golden eyes, for he was well aware that his grandmother was eager for him to take a wife. 'With all due respect, *Abuela*…I don't think that a sacrifice of that magnitude will be necessary.'

'A baby needs a mother. I'm too old to take on the role and the staff cannot be expected to fill the gap. You travel a great deal,' Doña Ernesta reminded him. 'Only a wife could ensure the continuing level of care and affection which a young child will require.'

As Antonio listened the amusement slowly evaporated from his gaze. 'I don't need a wife.'

Glancing up without apparent concern, Doña Ernesta treated her grandson to an understanding smile. 'Then, I can only offer you my admiration. Obviously you've already thought this matter over—'

'I have and in depth,' Antonio slotted in rather drily, for he was unimpressed by his wily grandmother's pretence of innocence.

'And you're prepared to sacrifice all your free time for your niece's benefit. After all, with only you to depend on, she will need so much more of your attention.'

That angle had not occurred to Antonio. His brilliant eyes grew bleak. He was most reluctant to contemplate that level of commitment. He could not imagine assuming the role of a hands-on parent in constant demand. The very idea of such a thing was ridiculous. He was the Marqués de Salazar, head of an ancient and noble family line, as well as being a powerful and influential businessman on whom many thousands of employees depended. His time was too valuable. His importance to the success of his business projects was limitless. What did he know about children? Babies?

At the same time the very idea of embracing the imprisonment of marriage banged the equivalent of a sepulchral cell door shut in Antonio's imagination and made him pale.

In the act of changing Lydia's T-shirt, Sophie succumbed to temptation and blew a raspberry on her niece's tummy. Convulsing with chuckles, Lydia held up her arms to be lifted, her little face below her soft brown curls lit by a sunny smile.

'I don't know which one of you is the bigger kid!'

Norah Moore quipped while her stocky, well-built son, Matt, set the old highchair out beside the pine kitchen table.

Tiny in stature and slender as a ribbon, Sophie thrust her own curls back off her brow in a rueful gesture and resisted the urge to admit that grief, stress and a heavy workload were combining to make her feel more like a hundred years old. Staying financially afloat was a constant struggle and since Lydia's birth had required her to do two jobs. Her main income came from working as a cleaner for the Moores. Mother and son owned the trailer park where she had lived for almost four years. At present she cleaned the caravans that were rented out as holiday lets. But quite a few were lived in all the year round by people like herself who could not afford more expensive accommodation. She made extra cash from embroidering clothes for an exclusive mail order firm. Her earnings might be poor in comparison to the hours she put in but she was grateful for any work that she could combine with caring for Lydia.

'But I know which one of you is the prettiest,' Matt declared with a meaningful look in Sophie's direction.

As Sophie strapped Lydia into the high chair she contrived to evade his admiring gaze and wondered why Mother Nature was always encouraging the wrong men to chase her. She liked Matt. She had tried, she really had tried to find him attractive because he was hardworking, honest and decent. He was everything her irresponsible father had not been and a solid gold choice for a sensible woman. As always she wished that she were less fanciful and more prudent.

'Right now, I should think Sophie's more concerned about what this solicitor might have to say to her,' Norah, a thin woman with short grey hair, told her son brusquely. 'I can't understand why Belinda even bothered to make a will when she had nothing to leave.'

'She had Lydia,' Sophie pointed out to the older woman. 'Belinda had the will drawn up after Pablo died. I think it must've been her way of making a new start and showing her independence.'

'Yes, your sister was very keen on her independence,' Norah Moore said with a sniff. 'And not so fond of being tied down to a kiddie once Lydia was born.'

'It was hard for her.' Sophie lifted a slight shoulder in a noncommittal shrug because it hurt that she could not actively defend Belinda's rash behaviour during the last months of her life. At least, not to a woman who had repeatedly helped her out with the task of caring for Belinda's daughter. But then that was what she most liked about the Moores, she reminded herself. They spoke as they found and there was nothing false about them.

'It was even harder for you,' Norah told her squarely. 'I felt very sorry for Belinda when she first came here. She'd had a tough time. But when she took up with that new boyfriend of hers and landed you with Lydia, I lost patience with her silliness.'

'I loved being landed with Lydia,' Sophie declared staunchly.

'Sometimes what you love may not be what's good for you,' the older woman retorted crisply.

But at a time when Sophie's heart still ached from the cruelly sudden death of her sister, her baby niece was her only real comfort. Although Sophie and Belinda had had different fathers and had not met until Belinda had sought Sophie out. Sophie had grown very fond of her older sister. Belinda had, after all, shown Sophie the first family affection that the younger woman had ever known.

Yet the stark difference between their respective backgrounds might more easily have ensured that the two sisters remained lifelong strangers. While Belinda had grown up in a lovely country house with her own pony and every childhood extra her parents could afford, Sophie had been born illegitimate and raised in a council flat by a father who was always broke. Sophie was the result of their mother, Isabel's extramarital affair. After her infatuation had subsided, Isabel had won her estranged husband back by leaving Sophie behind with her lover. Sophie's feckless father had brought her up with the help of a succession of girlfriends. She had learned when she was very young that her wants and wishes were rarely of interest to the self-seeking adults who surrounded her.

At first meeting, Sophie had been in awe of her beautiful, sophisticated sister. Five years older, Belinda had been educated at a fancy boarding-school and she had talked with a cut glass accent that put Sophie in mind of the royal family. Her warm and affectionate nature had however soon won Sophie's trust and love. Perhaps more slowly and rather more painfully, Sophie had come to appreciate that Belinda was not very clever and was extremely vulnerable to falling for handsome men who talked big and impressed her. But wild horses would have not have dredged that unhappy truth from Sophie, who was loyal to a fault.

Leaving her niece in Norah Moore's capable care, Sophie climbed into Matt's pick-up. He gave her a lift into Sheerness and, stopping right outside the solicitor's office, he offered to wait for her.

As always in a hurry to escape Matt's hopeful air of

expectation, Sophie had already jumped out onto the pavement. 'There's no need,' she said breezily. 'I'll catch the bus.'

Matt behaved as if she hadn't spoken and told her where he would be parked.

A young car driver waiting at the lights buzzed down his window to call, 'Hiya, sexy!'

Sophie flung him a pained glance from eyes as deep and rich and green as old-fashioned bottle glass. 'Shouldn't you be in school?'

He looked startled by the comeback. Sophie pondered the decided embarrassment of still looking like a sixteen-year-old when she was almost twenty-three years old. She blamed her youthful appearance on her lack of height and skinny build. She kept her hair long because, although she would not have admitted it to a living soul, she was always terrified that her slender curves might lead to her being mistaken for a boy.

As she entered the legal firm's smart office she tugged uneasily at the hem of her denim skirt, which rejoiced in floral cotton frills. The skirt was well out of fashion and she had worn it only because she thought it looked more formal than the jeans that filled her limited wardrobe. All her clothes came from charity shops and none were of the designer cast-off variety. Without complaint, she hovered while the receptionist chatted to a colleague and answered a call before finally deigning to take note of her arrival.

In the waiting room, Sophie took up a restive position by the window. She watched a limousine force its passage along the street outside and cause traffic chaos. The long silver vehicle came to a halt and a uniformed chauffeur emerged. Impervious to the car horns that protested the obstruction that the limo was creating, he opened a rear door for his passenger to alight.

As the passenger sprang out and straightened to an imposing height the breath caught in Sophie's throat. Her green eyes widened with disbelief. It couldn't be, it simply couldn't be Pablo's autocratic big brother, Antonio Rocha! She shrank back to the side of the window but continued to stare. It was Antonio all right. He had the impact of a tidal wave on her self-command.

There he was: the male who had made mincemeat of her every prejudice, overpowered her defences and reduced her to a level of eyelash-fluttering, giggly compliance. She suppressed a quiver of shame at that recollection. For nearly three years since that awful day, Sophie had told herself that Antonio could not possibly have been half as devastatingly attractive as she had believed him to be. And now here he was in the flesh to destroy even that comforting lie with his smooth aristocratic façade that set her teeth on edge and his altogether more disturbing quality of raw sexuality.

His gleaming black hair was cut fashionably short. His lean, classic features were stamped with a bold masculinity that attracted female admiration wherever he went. He was a work of art, Sophie acknowledged grudgingly. Not only did he look like some mythical Greek god, he was also built like one with broad shoulders, a narrow waist and long, powerful legs. Dressed in a trendy dark designer suit, he looked achingly handsome. Only when he strode into the same legal practice did she break free of her paralysis and sincerely doubt the evidence of her own eyes.

Why would Antonio Rocha be over in England? What was he doing on the Isle of Sheppey where the titled rich were scarcer than hens' teeth? Surely he could only be in Sheerness on this particular day to keep the same appointment that she had been asked to attend? No other reason could rationally explain such a coincidence.

Sophie hurried over to the door that led back into the reception area where an alarming amount of activity had broken out. The once laconic receptionist was standing to attention with a megawatt smile of appreciation and a well-dressed older man was greeting Antonio with a horrendous amount of bowing and scraping. 'Your Excellency,' he murmured obsequiously.

As though some sixth sense warned him of her presence, Antonio turned his proud dark head. Eyes as rich as gold ingots in sunlight encountered hers. Her tummy flipped and her mouth ran dry and her heartbeat escalated as though she were trying to run up a hill. It was like being hit by a truck at breakneck speed and she reacted with panic.

'Just what the heck are *you* doing here?' Sophie asked belligerently.

Taken aback though Antonio was by her unexpected appearance, he betrayed no visible sign of the fact. In the space of a moment, he had absorbed every facet of the slender woman poised by the door. She had the fine bones and grace of a dancer and the transient air of a butterfly ready to take wing at the first sign of trouble. Her toffee-blonde hair fell in a riotous mass of curls round her delicately pointed face, framing wide green eyes bright and sharp as lancets, a freckled nose turned up at the tip and a full sweet cupid's bow mouth. His keen gaze semi-cloaked by the lush density of his lashes, he tore his attention from the provocative appeal of that very feminine mouth and struggled to suppress a primitive and infuriatingly inappropriate flare of pure lust.

Sophie folded her arms to hide the fact that her hands were shaking. 'I asked you a question, Antonio—who asked you to come here?' she demanded.

'His Excellency is attending this meeting at my request, Miss Cunningham,' the solicitor interposed in a shocked tone of reproof.

Antonio moved a step closer and extended both his lean brown hands. His stunning dark deep-set eyes met hers in a head-on collision. Before she even knew what she was doing she was uncrossing her defensive arms and freeing her fingers to make contact with him, for a yearning she could not deny had leapt up inside her.

'I know how close you were to your sister. Allow me to offer you my deepest condolences on her death,' Antonio breathed with quiet gravity.

Hot colour rose like a flood tide to wash Sophie's pale complexion. Her small hands trembled in the warm hold of his. Ferocious emotions gripped her and threatened to tear her apart. She could not doubt his sincerity and his compassion pushed her to the brink of tears. With his immaculate sense of occasion, social sophistication and superb manners, he had put her in the wrong by answering her less-than-polite greeting with courtesy. For that alone, Sophie could have screamed at him and wept in rage. She refused to be impressed. She also refused to think about how much he had hurt her almost three years earlier. Instead she concentrated on a more relevant line of attack. Where had Antonio Rocha and his rich, snobby family been when Belinda had been desperate for help and support?

She jerked her hands free in stark rejection. 'I don't want your precious condolences!' she told him baldly.

'Nonetheless they are yours,' Antonio purred smoothly, marvelling at the level of her aggression and the novelty value of her rebuff. Women were never aggressive towards Antonio or ungrateful for his consideration. Sophie was the single exception to that rule.

'You still haven't told me what you're doing here,' Sophie said stubbornly.

'I was invited,' Antonio reminded her gently.

'Your Excellency…please come this way,' the solicitor urged him in a pained tone of apology.

Although Sophie had grown increasingly pale with discomfiture and nerves, her chin came up. 'I'm not going anywhere until someone tells me what's going on! What gives you the right to hear what my sister said in her will?'

'Let's discuss that and other issues in a more private setting,' Antonio suggested quietly.

Once again Sophie's face flamed pink with chagrin. Squirming embarrassment afflicted her when she unwillingly recalled the consequences of her visit to Spain nearly three years earlier. His rejection had hurt like hell and devastated her pride. She had been too pathetically naïve to recognise that the blue-blooded Marqués de Salazar was simply amusing himself with a bit of a flirtation. It was an effort for her to repress that wounding memory and concentrate on the present.

Her slender spine stiff, she sank down in a seat in the spacious office. Determined to emulate Antonio's cool, she resolved to resist the temptation to give way to any further outbursts and she compressed her lips. At the same time she was frantically striving to work out why Antonio Rocha should have been asked to come all the way from Spain. After all, Pablo's haughty brother had not bothered to get in touch before, nor had he shown the smallest interest in the existence of his infant niece. An enervating frisson of anxiety travelled through Sophie.

The solicitor began to read the will with the slight haste of someone eager to get an unpleasant task out of the way. The document was short and simple and all too soon Sophie understood why Antonio's presence had been deemed necessary. However, she could not accept what she had heard and questioned it. 'My sister nominated Antonio as a guardian as well?'

'Yes,' the solicitor confirmed.

'But I'm more than capable of taking care of Lydia,' Sophie proclaimed brightly. 'So there's no need for anyone else to get involved!'

'It's not quite that simple,' Antonio Rocha slotted in smooth as a rapier blade, but a faint frown line now divided his ebony brows. He was surprised that the will had made no mention of the disposition of Belinda's property and was about to query that omission.

Sophie spared the tall Spaniard her first fleeting glance since entering the room. Her troubled green eyes telegraphed a storm warning. 'It can be as simple as you're willing to make it. I don't know what came over Belinda when she chose to include you—'

'Common sense?' Antonio batted back drily.

'I suppose Belinda must've been scared that both her and me might be involved in an accident,' Sophie opined heatedly, fingers of pink highlighting her tautening facial bones as she fought to maintain her composure. 'We're talking worst-case scenario here, but luckily things aren't as bad as that. I'm young and fit and well able to take care of Lydia all on my own.'

'I would take issue with that statement,' Antonio murmured.

Her teeth gritted. 'You can take issue with whatever you like but it's not going to change anything!' she shot back at him.

'Your sister nominated you and the marqués as joint guardians of her daughter,' the solicitor expanded. 'That means that you have equal rights over the child—'

'Equal rights?' Sophie gasped in rampant disbelief.

'Equal rights,' Antonio repeated with a silken emphasis he could not resist.

'No other arrangement is possible without application to the courts,' the solicitor decreed.

'But that's utterly outrageous!' Sophie launched at Antonio.

'With all due respect, I would suggest that my family is entitled to assist in the task of raising my brother's child to adulthood.'

'Why?' Sophie slung back wrathfully as she leapt to her feet. 'So that your precious family can make as big a mess of bringing up Lydia as they did with her father?'

Angry disconcertion had tensed Antonio's lean, darkly handsome features. 'Both our siblings are now dead. Let us respect that reality.'

'Don't you dare ask me to respect Pablo's memory!' Sophie flared back at him in disgust. 'Your brother wrecked my sister's life!'

'May I speak to Miss Cunningham alone for a few minutes?' Antonio enquired of the solicitor.

The older man, whose discomfiture during that increasingly heated exchange of views had been extreme, got up with relief at the request and left the room.

'Sit down,' Antonio instructed coolly, determined not to rise to the bait of her provocative accusations. 'Appreciate that I will not argue with you. Recriminations are pointless and wrong in this situation. The child's interests must come first—'

Sophie was so furious that only a scream could have expressed her feelings. Denied that outlet, she coiled her hands into tight little fists of restraint by her side. 'Don't you dare tell me what's right and what's wrong. Let me tell you—'

Antonio rose upright with unhurried grace. 'You will tell me nothing that I do not ask for, as I will not listen. You will lower your voice and moderate your language.'

'Where do you get off talking to me like that? Like I'm some stupid kid?' Sophie launched at him. 'You walk in here, you start laying down the law and acting like you know best—'

'I most probably do know best,' Antonio incised and not in a tone of apology. 'I recognise that you have suffered a recent bereavement and that grief may well have challenged your temper—'

'That's not why I hate your guts and that is not why I am shouting at you!' Sophie informed him fiercely, green eyes bright with fury. 'Your rotten brother robbed my sister of everything she possessed and left her penniless and in debt. He was a hateful liar and a cheat. He took her money and threw it away at the gambling tables and at the racetrack. When there was nothing left he told her he'd never loved her anyway and he walked!'

Antonio was perturbed but not that surprised by those revelations. He felt it would be tactless to point out that, even before Belinda had wed his brother, he had made an unsuccessful attempt to warn Sophie's sibling of her future husband's essential unreliability when it came to money. 'If that is the truth I am sorry for it. Had I been made aware of those facts, I would have granted Belinda all the help that it was within my power to give.'

Sophie snatched in a jagged breath. 'Is that all you have got to say?'

Antonio had a low tolerance threshold for such personal attacks. In his blood ran the hot pure-bred pride of the Spanish nobility and a long line of ancestors to whom honour had been a chivalrous, engrained concept of prime importance. He had lived his own life within those tenets and his principles were of the highest. He had a profound dislike of being upbraided for his brother's sins, for which he had too often paid a high personal price. His strong jaw line squared. He had no intention of getting dragged into an exchange that was only likely to exacerbate hostilities.

'It is an unhappy fact that I cannot change the past,' Antonio pointed out flatly. 'The only subject I'm willing to discuss at this moment is your niece's well-being.'

Eyes glinting a ferocious green, Sophie surveyed him in raging frustration. Nothing fazed him. Nothing knocked even a chip off that cold, smooth, marble façade of his. He was neither shamed nor affronted by his younger brother's appalling mistreatment of her poor sister. Indeed there he stood, all six feet three inches of him, wonderfully insulated by his great wealth and aristocratic detachment from the harder realities of those less fortunate in life. He lived in a castle with servants. He had a private jet and a fleet of limos. His fancy suit had probably cost as much as she earned in a year. He would never know what it was to struggle just to pay the rent at the end of the month. He had even less compassion to spare for Belinda's sufferings.

'I'm not going to discuss Lydia with you!' Sophie

snapped in the feverish heat of her resentment. 'You're as much of a bastard as your sneaky brother was!'

Dark colour accentuated the superb slant of Antonio's fabulous cheekbones. His brilliant eyes suddenly flared gold as the heart of a fire. 'On what do you base your abuse? Ignorant prejudice?'

'I've got personal experience of what kind of a guy you are!' Sophie declared in a tempestuous surge of hurt and anger. 'Not my type anyway!'

'Sorry, I'm just not into tattoos,' Antonio murmured in a sibilant tone designed to wound.

'Tattoos?' Sophie parroted in response to that particular taunt, feeling the image of the butterfly she had acquired at eighteen burn through the flesh of her shoulder like a brand. A fresh spurt of angry mortification took hold of her. 'You total snob and snake! How dare you sneer at me like that? You act like you're so superior and so polite, but you strung me a line and let me down and misjudged me that night!'

Antonio's intent dark golden gaze was welded to her flushed heart-shaped face and bright green eyes. Her passion fascinated him. Temper was running through her like an electric current and she could not control it. He was grimly amused and unexpectedly pleased to discover that his justifiable put-down that night still rankled with her nearly three years after the event.

'I don't think so. I think you resent the fact that I saw you for what you were—'

Sophie was trembling with the force of her feelings. 'And how did you see me?' she challenged.

'You don't want to know,' Antonio asserted lazily, dangling that carrot with every hope of provoking her further. She was already so mad she was practically jumping up and down on the spot and he could not resist the temptation to see just how much further he could push her before she lost it altogether.

Sophie took a hasty step closer and stared up at him with outrage stamped in her delicate features, her hands on her hips like a miniature fishwife. 'Tell me…go on, just tell me!'

Antonio lifted and dropped his wide shoulders in an infinitesimal shrug of dismissal, deliberately prolonging the moment to the punchline. 'In common with most men, I confess that I can really enjoy a wanton woman, but I'm afraid that promiscuity is a real turn-off. You missed your chance with me.'

Sophie hit him. She tried to slap him, but she was not tall enough. His reactions were also faster than her own and he sidestepped her so that her palm merely glanced off his shoulder, leaving him infuriatingly unharmed. 'You pig!' she seethed up at him. 'You think I care about missing out with you?'

'Attempted assault on that score nearly three years later rather speaks for you, *querida*,' Antonio shared in his dark-timbred drawl, only dimly wondering why he was enjoying himself so much.

White with shock and chagrin at her own behaviour and the biting effect of his derision, Sophie headed to the door. 'I refuse to have anything more to do with you.'

'Perhaps just once you could exercise some discipline over your temper and think of the child whose future is at stake here.'

Sophie froze as if his words had plunged a dagger into her narrow back. Guilt and shame engulfed her. Stiffly she turned and tracked back to her seat without once looking in the direction of her tormentor.

'Thank you,' Antonio Rocha murmured smoothly.

Her fingers carved purple crescents of restraint into her palms. Never in her life had she hated anyone as she hated him at that moment. Never in her life had anyone made her feel so stupid and selfish. He invited the solicitor back in. Initially she was silent for fear of letting herself down by saying the wrong thing, but she had been planning to ask questions. However, there was no need for her to do so. Antonio requested the clarification that she might have asked for her own benefit and the answers told a chastened Sophie what she least wished to hear.

All arrangements for Lydia would have to be reached by mutual agreement between her and Antonio. Either of them could refuse the responsibility or relinquish rights to the other. But, as executor, the solicitor was empowered, if he thought it necessary, to invite social services to decide how Lydia's needs would best be fulfilled. Adequate security and funding to support a child would naturally have to be taken into consideration.

'So as I'm poor and Antonio's rich, I can't possibly have equal rights with him over my niece, can I?' Sophie prompted tightly.

'That is not how I would view the situation, Miss Cunningham.' Dismayed by such blunt speech, the solicitor glanced at Antonio for support.

Antonio Rocha, Marqués de Salazar, rose unhurriedly upright a split second after Sophie scrambled to her feet, eager to be gone. 'I see no reason why Miss Cunningham and I should not reach an amicable agreement,' he drawled with all the controlled calm and cool of a male who knew he had beaten an opponent hollow. 'I'd like to see Lydia this evening. Shall we say at seven? I'll call at your home.'

'I'm sure you're not giving me a choice,' Sophie framed bitterly.

Having taken complete charge, Antonio accompanied her out to the narrow corridor. 'It doesn't have to be this way between us,' he murmured huskily.

'How else could it be?' she heard herself prompt.

He was so close that she could have reached out and touched him. The very sound of his rich, deep-pitched drawl was incredibly sensual. She let herself look up and it was a mistake. He took her breath away and rocked her world on its axis. In the blink of an eyelid it was as though time had slipped and catapulted her back almost three years. Meeting the slumberous darkness of his spectacular eyes, she trembled. Treacherous excitement seized her and made a prisoner of her. For a wild, endless moment, she was so fiercely aware of him that it was agony not to make actual physical contact with his lean, powerful frame. She heard the roughened catch of his breathing and imagined the burn of his beautiful mouth on hers. Only the humiliating memory of his comments earlier forced her back to solid earth again and left her bitterly ashamed of her own weakness.

'Do you honestly think I'm stupid enough to fall for the same fake charm routine you used on me the last time?' Sophie asked with stinging scorn, sliding sinuously past him with the quicksilver speed that characterised all her movements. She had vanished round the corner at the foot of the corridor before he was even properly aware that she had gone.

Antonio swore long and low and silently and with a ferocity that would have astounded those who knew him.

CHAPTER TWO

ON THE drive back home, Sophie gave Matt a brief update on events and then fell silent. She was too upset to make conversation.

Shattered by the contents of Belinda's will, Sophie was simply terrified that she was in serious danger of losing Lydia and shell-shocked by meeting up with Antonio Rocha again. How could her sister have chosen Antonio to be her child's guardian? After all, Belinda had had virtually no contact with her Spanish in-laws after her wedding. She had once admitted to Sophie that Pablo had never got on with his relatives and that that was why he preferred to live in London. When Antonio had contacted Belinda after Pablo's death, Belinda had been almost hysterical in her determination to have nothing further to do with her late husband's family. Even when Belinda had mentioned the will she had made, she had not admitted to Antonio's place in it. Sophie had been totally unprepared for her sibling's evident change of heart.

Nevertheless, Sophie could also understand exactly why Antonio had been selected: Belinda had always had enormous respect for money and status. It was rather ironic that her sister had actually been rather intimidated by the sheer grandeur of her husband's family, who lived on a palatial scale. She thought that Belinda had most probably been hedging her bets when she had named Antonio in the will. Knowing that Sophie was poor as a church mouse, she could only have hoped that including the mega-rich Antonio might result in his offering to contribute towards his niece's support. Sophie clutched at that concept and prayed that Pablo's brother would have no desire to become any more closely involved in Lydia's life.

Sophie had come to love Lydia as much as if her niece had been born to her. The bond between Sophie and her infant niece would always have been strong because, having suffered leukaemia as a child, Sophie was painfully aware that the treatment that had saved her life might also have left her infertile. Her attachment to her sister's baby had been intensified, however, by the simple fact that from birth Lydia had been almost solely in Sophie's care.

Initially Belinda had not been well and she had needed Sophie to look after her daughter until she was stronger. Within a few weeks, though, Belinda had met the man with whom she had been living at the time of her death. A successful salesman with a party-going lifestyle, Doug had shown no interest whatsoever in his girlfriend's baby. Having fallen for him, Belinda had been quick to pass all responsibility for Lydia onto Sophie's shoulders.

On many occasions, Sophie had attempted to reason with her sister and persuade her to spend more time with her baby daughter.

'I wish I'd never had her!' Belinda finally sobbed shamefacedly. 'If I have to start playing Mummy and staying in more, Doug will just find someone else. I know I'm not being fair to you but I love him so much and I don't want to lose him. Just give me some more time with him. I know he'll come round about Lydia.'

But Doug did not come round. Indeed he told Belinda that there was no room for a child in his life.

'That's why I've reached a decision,' Belinda told Sophie tearfully two weeks before she died. 'You probably can't have a baby of your own and I know how much you love Lydia. You've been a terrific mother to her, much better than I could ever be. If you want Lydia, you can keep her for ever and that way I can at least see her occasionally.'

That day Sophie deemed it wisest to say nothing, for she was convinced that Belinda's affair with Doug was already fading and that her sister would soon bitterly regret her willingness to sacrifice even her child on his behalf. Sophie had grown up in a household where her father's lady friends had almost always had children of their own. She knew that there were plenty of men who refused to take responsibility for anyone other than their own sweet selves. Her father had been one of that ilk, a work-shy charmer of colossal selfishness, but he had never been without a woman in his life. All too often those same women had put his needs ahead of their child's in a pointless effort to hold on to him.

'My goodness...fancy Belinda not even telling you!' Norah Moore exclaimed in astonishment when she heard about Antonio Rocha's appearance at the solicitor's office. 'That sister of yours was a dark horse, all right.'

Engaged in cuddling Lydia close and rejoicing in the sweet, soft warmth of her niece's weight in her arms, Sophie sighed, 'Belinda probably put Antonio's name down and never thought about it again. She didn't keep secrets from me.'

'Didn't she?' the older woman snorted, unimpressed. 'I reckon Belinda only ever told you what she thought you wanted to hear!'

Sophie stiffened. 'What's that supposed to mean? Are you teasing me?'

Reddening, Norah looked discomfited. 'Of course I am,' she said awkwardly.

It was not the first time that the older woman had hinted that Sophie might not have known her sibling as well as she thought she did. Sophie was irritated but placed no credence in that suggestion. She was well aware that Norah and Belinda had merely tolerated each other. Norah had been too rough and ready for Belinda's refined standards and had been hurt and offended by the younger woman's coolness.

With Lydia in her pram, Sophie left the Moores' neat little bungalow and walked back to the static caravan where she lived. Belinda had totally loathed living there and had been delighted to move into her boyfriend's smart apartment in town. But Sophie looked on the caravan as her home and loved the fact that the big front window looked out on a field where sheep sometimes grazed. Indeed, high on her agenda was the dream that some day she might be in a position to stop renting and buy a more up-to-date model.

Changing back into her jeans and gathering up her cleaning materials, Sophie was in a hurry to make up the time she had lost from her day's work. Try as she might, she found it impossible to lock her memories of Belinda's wedding and her first meeting with Antonio out of her thoughts…

Sophie had been thrilled when she was asked to be a bridesmaid. Some of her enthusiasm had waned, however, once she'd realised that Belinda wanted her to conceal her humble beginnings and avoid any close contact with Pablo's blue-blooded family. Only her sister's frantic pleas for her to share that special day with her had persuaded Sophie to overlook those embarrassing strictures.

Belinda had paid all her expenses and it had been cheapest for Sophie to travel to Spain on a five-day package holiday at a nearby resort. Sophie's father, his then girlfriend and her son had decided to take advantage of the low prices and share the same apartment. The day of their arrival, and the night before the wedding, Sophie had accompanied Belinda to a social evening at the imposingly large home of one of Pablo's relatives.

Sophie had felt like a prune in the fancy pink suit that Belinda had insisted on buying for her. Worried that she might mortify her sister by saying or doing the wrong thing in such exalted company, Sophie had taken refuge in the billiards room. It was there that she had met Antonio for the first time. Glancing up from the solo game she had been engaged in, she had seen him watching her from the doorway. Drop-dead gorgeous in an open-necked black shirt and chinos, he had simply taken her breath away.

'How long have you been standing there?' she asked.

Antonio laughed huskily. 'Long enough to appreciate your skill,' he replied in perfect, accented English. 'But you're not playing billiards, you're playing snooker. Who taught you?'

'My dad.'

'Either you're a born player or you must have practised a great deal.'

Sophie resisted the urge to admit that when she was a kid her father had often kept her out of school so that he could take her into bars at lunchtime and place bets on her ability to beat all comers at snooker. Her father had only stopped that lucrative pastime when the authorities had given him a stern warning about her poor school-attendance record.

'I guess…' she muttered, biting her lower lip while all the while studying him from below her lashes and feeling horribly shy. She had an innate distrust of handsome men and he was dazzling. She was also noticing the subtle signs of expensive designer elegance in his apparel and going into automatic retreat. 'I shouldn't be in here.'

'Why not? Are you not a friend of the bride's?'

Remembering Belinda's warning, she nodded grudging agreement.

'And your name?' Antonio prompted, strolling silently closer.

'Sophie…'

He extended a lean brown hand. 'I am Antonio.'

Awkwardly she brushed his fingertips and backed towards the door. 'I'd better get back to the other room before I'm missed. I don't want to insult them—'

'Them…?' He quirked an amused dark brow. 'All those terrifying Spanish people next door?'

'It might seem funny to you, but I don't speak the lingo and the ones that speak English can't seem to understand *my* English and keep on asking me to repeat things… It's a nightmare!' she heard herself confiding, desperately grateful just to find someone who could follow what she was saying.

'I shall go and tell them off immediately. How dare they frighten you into hiding in the billiard room?' Antonio teased.

Sophie lifted her chin. 'I don't hide from people.'

'Let's play…' He presented her with the cue she had abandoned. 'I'll teach you the game.'

'I'll beat you hollow,' she warned him.

His stunning dark eyes gleamed with pleasure at that unashamed challenge to his masculinity. 'I don't think so.'

In fact she played the worst she had ever played. She was so intensely aware of him that she was quite unable to resist the need to keep on looking across at him. She was terrified of the strength of his attraction for her. Young though she was, she was painfully aware of the havoc that tended to result from such wayward physical enthusiasms. It was almost a relief when Belinda interrupted them, aghast to find her little sister in Antonio's company. Making an excuse, Belinda was quick to separate them.

'Didn't you realise who he is?' she scolded Sophie. 'You shouldn't even be talking to him. That's Pablo's big brother…the one with the title and the castle… the Marqués of Salazar.'

For a real live Spanish marquis, Antonio had, on first brief acquaintance at least, seemed refreshingly hip and normal. Sophie was savagely disappointed to discover how far he was out of her reach and annoyed that Antonio had not spelled out exactly who he was. Impervious to Belinda's clumsy attempts to keep them apart, Antonio intervened to sweep Sophie off to meet some of the younger people present. When the evening came to a close, it was Antonio who had to drive Sophie back to the holiday resort: in all the excitement of being the centre of attention as the bride, Belinda had forgotten about her sister's transport needs.

'I can't understand why you are not staying with your sister at my grandmother's home,' Antonio admitted, assisting her into a long, low-slung fire-engine-red sports car that would have looked at home in a Bond movie.

'I didn't want to intrude—'

'I'm not happy that you should be staying in an apartment alone. I do not wish to imply criticism of your sister, but you should be relaxing and enjoying my family's hospitality. I'll wait while you pack,' Antonio imparted with the quiet but absolute authority of a male accustomed to instant obedience to his every expressed wish.

'But I'm not alone...er, I'm with friends,' Sophie protested awkwardly, recognising the impossibility of naming her father when Belinda had begged her not to tell a living soul that they were actually only half-sisters because their late mother had had an extramarital affair. Her sibling had been ashamed of that history, had already refused to share it with Pablo and had been determined that his aristocratic relatives should not find out about it either.

'Friends?' Antonio queried, his bewilderment visibly growing.

'Yes, I decided to make a holiday out of my trip over here...nothing wrong with that, is there?'

'No, there is not,' Antonio drawled in a measured tone. 'But you only arrived in Spain this morning and are perhaps not the best judge of good accommodation. My cousin owns a local business and he tells me that the tourist complex where you are staying has a bad name. The police are often called there to deal with fights and drunks.'

She resisted a flippant urge to tell him that her father would be very much at home there. 'I'm not a delicate flower...I'll manage.'

'But you should not have to manage,' Antonio murmured gently.

The idea that she might look to a man to protect her

from the evils of the world was a really novel concept to Sophie. She lay awake that night on her uncomfortable sofa bed in the apartment's tiny reception area. While she strove to block out the noise of the argument between her father and his girlfriend in the room next door she discovered that she could not stop thinking about Antonio.

At every point where she had consciously expected Antonio to reveal his male feet of clay, she had been confounded. He had listened to every little thing she'd said as if he was interested. He had not once shouted at her or sworn at her or eyed up other girls. He did not drink and drive. Nor had he at any stage attempted to ply her with alcohol or make a pass at her. Indeed Antonio Rocha had in some mysterious and romantic way contrived to make Sophie feel special and cosseted and worthy of attention and care for the first time ever.

At twenty years old, Sophie had never had a serious boyfriend. She was a virgin because she was totally terrified of sliding down the same slippery slope that had wrecked the lives of most of her father's girlfriends. Unlike them, she hadn't had to worry about becoming a mother at too young an age. But she had observed that placing faith and energy in countless casual relationships could result in low self-esteem, even a disrupted education and poor employment prospects, thus trapping one in poverty. She had told herself that she was too clever to succumb to the dangerous allure of casual sex, but the real truth was that she had never been remotely tempted to succumb to the coarse advances she had met with.

Never before had she lain awake until dawn counting the hours until she would see a guy again. Never before had she agonised over whether or not a man liked her or whether in fact he was simply being polite. Never before had she fantasised like mad over what it would be like if that same man were to kiss her. In fact her imagination was so extravagantly exercised by Antonio that when she saw him face to face again embarrassment afflicted her with blushes, stammers and painful shyness for the first time in her life. She had floated through Belinda's wedding festivities on a cloud of such intense happiness that the wake-up call of cruel reality had been all the harder to bear twenty-four hours later…

Antonio stayed behind at the solicitor's to clarify certain matters for his own benefit. Even the vague facts that he was able to establish stamped the kind of reflective frown to his lean, dark features that put his employees on their mettle.

Evidently, Belinda had been penniless at the time of her death and working as a barmaid. Yet when she had married Pablo, the beautiful blonde had been a receptionist in a London modelling agency, her comfort and security ensured by the healthy amount of cash and property she had inherited from her parents. Antonio had little need to wonder who or what had been responsible for bringing about Belinda's reduced circumstances and angry regret gripped him. That his late sister-in-law had been living with another man did go some way to satisfying his need to know why Belinda had apparently been determined not to ask her late husband's family for help.

It took a lot to shock Antonio but he was stunned when, having asked for Sophie's address, he learned where exactly she was living. He could not initially credit that she resided in a trailer park. Was his criminally dishonest brother responsible for her impoverishment as well? The limousine paused outside the entrance while his chauffeur double-checked his destination with his employer. Alighting outside the run-down office, Antonio decided that Sophie was a problem best cured by the liberal application of money.

Sophie was cleaning the floor in one of the smarter mobile homes on the site when a brisk knock sounded on the door. Scrambling up, she pushed it open and froze when she clashed with dark-as-midnight eyes set below level black brows. She knew she should not but she stared, drinking in the dark, sexy symmetry of his bold, masculine features. Her heart started to beat very, very fast. 'You said seven o'clock,' she reminded him. 'What are you doing here this early?'

'Is this not a good time for you?' Antonio enquired, his keen gaze raking from the torrent of her curls gilded to gold by the sunlight to the vivid intensity of her animated face and then back to centre on the soft, ripe curve of her mouth. Taken individually her features were ordinary and flawed, he reflected grimly. But that did not explain why she continually gave him the impression of being ravishingly pretty.

'No, it's not… I mean, I'm working and Lydia's asleep and it's just not convenient,' Sophie broke into an enervated surge of protest.

'I appreciate that but I have nothing else to do in this locality while I wait. I'm also understandably eager to meet my niece,' Antonio responded without apology. There was a brooding coolness in his decisive scrutiny as he suppressed the absurd spark of desire she always generated. He could only think she had the deceptive allure of the unfamiliar for him. 'May I come in?'

Feeling ridiculously flustered, Sophie edged back into the trailer's small lounge area and surreptitiously moistened her dry mouth. He strolled up the steps and took up what felt like every square inch of space.

'You'll have to wait until Lydia wakes up from her nap.'

Impatience tautened Antonio's striking bone structure. 'Meeting her uncle should be rather more fun than sleeping. I haven't got much time to spend in the UK. I'd be grateful if you tried not to make matters more complicated than they need be.'

By the end of that little speech Sophie was breathing a little heavily. She had put Lydia down for a nap so that the baby would be less tired when Antonio made his visit. His early arrival had thrown that schedule into chaos. Her small, slight body stiff with annoyance and concern, she bent her curly head and pinned her lips tight on the tart comments eager to flow from her ready tongue. Antonio Rocha, Marqués of Salazar, was loaded. The solicitor had treated him like royalty and had treated her like trash to be tolerated. The warning was clear: she could not afford to make Antonio a bitter enemy. If push came to shove, he would always win the upper hand by virtue of his wealth and status. Therefore, even if it choked her, she had to be polite for Lydia's sake and swallow Antonio's every demand with as much grace as she could manage.

'Lydia will be a little cranky if we waken her before she's ready,' Sophie said hesitantly.

'I want to see my niece now,' Antonio decreed, having decided that Sophie responded best to firm authority.

After a pause for consideration, Sophie nodded, for she wanted to be fair. There had been a lot of little boys and girls at Belinda's wedding and her sister had once told her that the Spanish were particularly fond of children. Antonio was obviously accustomed to babies and confident of being able to handle his niece. She pushed open the door of the narrow bunkroom where she had stowed Lydia to sleep undisturbed in her little travel cot.

Antonio gazed down at the small hump under the blanket, which was topped by a fluff of light brown curls. His niece looked worryingly tiny. Both Pablo and Belinda had been tall. On the other hand Sophie barely reached the top of Antonio's chest, so it was perfectly possible that the baby was naturally undersized and still quite fit. He reminded himself that when he took Lydia back to Spain she would be checked over. The family doctor, who was an old friend, had suggested that giving the baby a full medical examination would be a wise precaution: one or two babies in the most recent generation had been born with heart murmurs.

Mastering his own reluctance, Antonio decided to show an appropriate level of interest in the child by lifting her out of the cot for a closer inspection. He brushed back the blanket and scooped the baby up.

Almost instantly, the baby went as stiff as a tiny steel girder and looked up at him with enormous stricken brown eyes. Her mouth opened wide enough to treat him to an unwelcome view of her miniature tonsils and a yell that would have roused a graveyard exploded from her. Her face turning scarlet, the baby shrieked blue murder as if she were being attacked. Antonio stared down at his niece in paralysed horror.

'What's wrong with her?' he demanded.

'Have you ever been snatched out of bed by a stranger and dangled in mid-air like a toy?' Sophie asked fiercely, resisting the urge to haul Lydia from his inept and unfeeling hands.

Hearing Sophie's voice, Lydia twisted her little head round. The baby squirmed like mad and stretched out her hands towards her aunt in a movement that was as frantic as it was revealing.

'Perhaps you should have made the effort to introduce us first,' Antonio censured, and without further ado he deposited the screaming bundle into Sophie's waiting arms.

His sculpted mouth curling, his ears still ringing from that appalling bout of shrieking, he watched his tiny niece clamp onto Sophie's shoulder like a limpet restored to its favourite rock. An immediate and very welcome silence fell. While the baby clung with what he considered to be quite unnecessary drama, Sophie rewarded that show of extreme favouritism with an enormous amount of petting and kissing and soothing whispers.

'I had no idea that the child would be quite so attached to you,' Antonio admitted flatly.

'I've been looking after Lydia since she was born.' Restless with tension, Sophie moved out of the bunkroom and back into the lounge. 'Belinda was ill at first…and then later, well, there were reasons why she wasn't able to spend as much time as she would have liked with her daughter.'

'What reasons?' Antonio prompted.

'Belinda started seeing a bloke who wasn't fussed about kids and when she moved in with him, Lydia stayed on with me,' Sophie explained grudgingly.

'Here…in this place?'

'We should be so lucky.' Sophie loosed an uneasy laugh. 'This is a luxury holiday home. The one I live in is at least twenty years older and without frills.'

Antonio spread his attention round the confines of a

room that he found claustrophobically small. Frills? What frills? The décor was abysmal and so jazzy and cheap it offended his eyes. *This* was what she called luxury? He bit back an incredulous comment.

'If you don't live in *this*, why are you here?'

'I'm cleaning it for the holiday-makers coming to stay tomorrow.'

Appalled by that admission, Antonio stared at her with concealed disbelief. 'You are employed on the park as a cleaner?'

Sophie curved Lydia even closer to her taut length. 'Have you got a problem with that?'

His strong jaw line squared, for he had hoped she had been joking. 'Of course not. You said that my brother robbed your sister. Did you lose money too?'

'I've never had money to lose,' Sophie answered in surprise, and then, realising that he did not understand why that should be the case, she sighed and surrendered to the inevitable. 'There's a skeleton in my family cupboard and Belinda didn't like me to talk about it. Belinda and I may have had the same mother but we had different fathers. I didn't meet my sister until I was seventeen.'

'All families have their secrets,' Antonio murmured, relieved to finally have some explanation on that score. 'Let us be candid with each other.'

Sophie tensed again. 'I wasn't going to tell you any lies.'

Picking up on her anxiety, Lydia lifted her head and loosed an uneasy little cry.

Antonio spread expressive lean brown hands. 'I do not want to argue with you.'

'Good...but between you and me and the wall there, you and I would always argue.'

'I don't accept that.' Antonio angled a smile at her, dark golden eyes cool and confident. 'A child's future is at stake here and after what you've undergone in recent months, it is natural that you should be under stress.'

'I haven't undergone anything,' Sophie asserted tightly. 'I love Lydia and I enjoy looking after her. Worrying about what's going to happen now that you're in the picture is all that's stressing me out.'

Two pairs of eyes, one green, one brown, were anxiously pinned to him, both fearful. For the first time in his thirty years of existence, Antonio felt like the wolf in the fairy tale, guilty of terrorising the innocent and the vulnerable. At the same time being treated like the bad guy infuriated him and stung his strong pride. He decided that it was time to drop the diplomatic approach. If he made his intentions and his expectations clear there would be no room for misunderstandings.

'Why should you worry about what's going to happen now that I'm here to help? I must assume that you intend to insult me—'

'No, I didn't intend that!' Sophie interrupted in dismay at that interpretation of her words.

Lean, strong face hard, Antonio dealt her a stony appraisal. 'My intervention can only be of advantage to my niece when she is currently living in appalling poverty. You have done your best in most trying circumstances and I honour you for your efforts on the child's behalf and thank you for your concern,' he drawled smooth as glass. 'But Lydia's best interests will be met only when I take her back to Spain and ensure that she receives the care and privileges which are hers by right of birth.'

As he spoke every atom of colour slowly drained

from Sophie's shattered face. 'We don't live in appalling poverty—'

'On my terms, I'm afraid that you do. I do not wish to offend you but I must speak the truth.'

'You can't take her away from me...and back to Spain,' Sophie breathed shakily, feeling so sick at that threat she could hardly squeeze out sound. The very idea of losing Lydia hit her as hard as a punch in the stomach, winding her, driving her mind blank with gut-wrenching fear.

'Why not?' Antonio quirked an ebony brow. She was white as snow and clutching the baby to her like a second skin. A mixture of frustration and anger gripped him, for he knew that his intentions were pure and his solution the only sensible one. 'I can see no alternative to that plan. If you love the child, you won't stand in her way. I will give her a much better life.'

Sophie took a step back as if she could no longer bear to be that close to him. 'I honestly think I will die if you take her away from me,' she framed unsteadily. 'I love her so much and she loves me. You can't just throw me out of her life as though I'm nothing just because I'm poor.'

Antonio stilled. Faint dark colour illuminated the spectacular slant of his carved cheekbones. He was severely disconcerted by the tears swimming in her eyes and her raw emotion. She had abandoned all pride, dropped her tough front. She looked like a tiny teenager striving to stand up to a bully. The baby, evidently picking up on her aunt's distress, was sobbing into Sophie's slight shoulder.

'It is not a matter of throwing you out of her life... This is the language of emotion, not of intellect,' Antonio censured in exasperation.

Sophie dragged in a deep, tremulous breath and treated him to a look of fierce condemnation. 'I'm not ashamed of that…as far as I'm concerned love would win over money every time—'

'According to what I understand, you've never had any money, so are scarcely qualified to make such a sweeping statement—'

'I love her…you don't!' Sophie launched at him.

'If you love her why don't you restrain your temper and stop scaring her?' Antonio asked with lethal effect.

Sophie gave him an anguished look and turned away, soothing the anxious child in her arms.

Antonio decided that it had been a definite mistake to try to cut to the baseline as if he were dealing with a business issue. There was nothing businesslike about Sophie. Nothing practical, nothing sensible, nothing controlled. In fact he had never seen a woman betray that amount of emotion and the freedom with which she showed it held an almost indecent fascination for him. She was a powder keg of passionate feeling. Sexual curiosity threatened to seize him and he fought it off, angry with her, angry with himself. But even anger could not make him unaware of a very powerful urge to just grab her up and flatten her to the nearest bed. Scarcely an appropriate response to her distress, he acknowledged. He despised the primitive reactions she had always stirred in him.

'I want you to think over what I've said,' Antonio continued, deciding that attempting further discussion in the current atmosphere would be unprofitable. 'I'll come back tomorrow morning at eleven. If you need to talk to me before then, you can reach me at this hotel.' He passed her a card. 'Tell me where you live.'

'In the blue van at the far end…the one parked right by the field,' Sophie told him chokily.

'I have no desire to sound like an actor in a bad movie but I can improve your life as well as Lydia's. You don't need to live at this level.'

'Oddly enough, I've never met any baby thieves living like this, only decent people who don't think money and social status is the be-all and end-all of life!' Sophie tossed back accusingly.

Antonio decided to prove his maturity by not responding to that taunt. 'I think it would be less upsetting for the baby if she was…resting when I call tomorrow.'

'Perhaps you'd like to think about how much Lydia will be upset if I suddenly vanish out of her life,' Sophie retorted thickly.

Antonio was sufficiently impressed by that warning to glance at the baby. He could not evade the suspicion that his brother's child had inherited Sophie's overly emotional temperament and was more sensitive than most. He had only lifted the child and it had gone off like a burglar alarm on hyper alert. For a split second he imagined carrying the baby away with both Sophie and the baby screaming and sobbing at high volume and he barely managed to repress a very masculine shudder.

Discovering a depth of imagination that he had not known he possessed, he even considered the risk of tabloid headlines and interference. *Baby thief.* No, he would be careful to do nothing likely to rouse such hysterical publicity. He was, he reminded himself, a highly intelligent and shrewd businessman. He was renowned for his logic and subtlety and his willingness to consider fresh and innovative approaches to find workable solutions. He was confident that he would find a way to persuade Sophie to accept the inevitable with good grace.

'You don't care about how I feel or how she feels, do you?' Sophie accused as she thrust wide the front door, descended the steps and proceeded to buckle Sophie into her buggy.

'I care enough to want to ensure that my niece does not grow up with your disadvantages.'

Shooting him a shocked glance from pain-filled green eyes, Sophie lifted her head high. 'Isn't it strange that even with all your advantages—your money and title and education and success—you are a ruthless bastard with no consideration for anyone's feelings but your own?'

Hot temper unleashing, Antonio surveyed her with thickly lashed eyes that shimmered a biting gold. 'But then I'm not a hypocrite. I know that you're not the fragile little flower that you look, *querida.* You're the same sleazy little liar who told me she was ill and then went out to get drunk and shag some loser on the beach,' he reminded her with icy derision. 'What you could never grasp about a guy like me is my good manners.'

'Excuse me? *You?* Good manners?' Sophie slung back at him in a hissing undertone selected to bypass Lydia's hearing.

'You said you were unwell. Naturally I went to see you to offer you my assistance.'

'Nah…that wasn't good manners, Antonio. You didn't trust me, so you called round to check up on me and you couldn't wait to jump to the wrong conclusions about me!' Sophie hurled with the bitterness she had never managed to shake off. 'Well, for your information, I told a polite lie to avoid embarrassing you with the truth of why I couldn't see you that night. And by the way, that loser you refer to was Terry, the son of my father's girlfriend, and he might have been very tall for his age but he was only fourteen years old! Not my lover, not my anything, just a scared kid worried sick about his mum!'

Having delivered that final rebuttal with spirit, Sophie stalked down the path with the buggy. To Antonio's eyes, she seemed to dance as she moved. Her golden corkscrew curls bounced and tumbled round her shoulders and down her narrow back. The worn fabric of her jeans accentuated the suggestion of a pert swing to her small, heart-shaped derrière. She did not have much of any particular attribute, but what she did have had an explosive effect on his libido. He was not proud of his base instincts. Willing his inappropriate arousal to hell and back, Antonio breathed in very slow and deep.

But he still wanted to haul her back and voice his scorn for that foolish story that only an intellectually challenged male would swallow. He wanted to ask her where she got off speaking to him in that impertinent tone. He wanted her to listen to his every word when he spoke to her. He wanted to teach her respect. He wanted to drag her into his arms and demonstrate sexual skills that he had never practised on a beach…at least, not a public one. Being who he was, however, and proud of his tough self-discipline, he chose instead to watch her walk away. He could no longer ignore the obvious: shameful though it was, it could only be her sluttish qualities that attracted him.

CHAPTER THREE

ANTONIO was planning to take Lydia from her and bring her up in Spain, Sophie reflected in agonised panic. How dared he start telling her how the baby that she loved should be brought up?

Frantically determined to keep herself busy so that she did not have time to fret, Sophie fed Lydia and put her to bed. She tidied up the static caravan that had been her home for over three years. She would make an early start tomorrow to finish that mobile home. She opened the box of cardigans the mail order firm had sent her to be embroidered and sat down to begin work on the intricate flowers.

How was she supposed to fight Antonio? A real live aristocrat? Was her lifestyle really one of appalling poverty? They had a secure roof over their heads and enough to eat. Admittedly the mobile home could be rather cold in winter and their clothes were rarely new, but Lydia was a happy, thriving child. How was she supposed to demand equal rights over her niece when Antonio could offer so much more in every material way?

Norah Moore called in at nine that evening. As soon as the older woman realised that Antonio was returning the next day, she offered to take care of Lydia while he was there. 'That way you'll be able to talk in peace. Where did you say this Antonio was staying?'

'I didn't say...the card's on the table,' Sophie mumbled, dimly wondering why the older woman wanted to know.

'Quite a way away...the hotel looks very fancy,' Norah remarked. 'You should take yourself off for a walk along the beach. That always calms you down. I'll mind Lydia.'

'How can I calm down? Antonio is going to take Lydia off me,' Sophie breathed in a tormented whisper. 'He's already made up his mind.'

'You can't be sure of that. Wait and see what happens. You might be surprised,' Norah remarked cryptically.

'I don't think so. Antonio was pretty blunt.'

The older woman gave Sophie's arm a comforting squeeze and departed without further comment.

Sophie trudged down to the beach and let the breeze toss her hair into a wild mass. Antonio had not changed one atom, she thought feverishly. He had not had a clue how to handle Lydia, but had been far too arrogant to admit it. In fact he appeared to know precious little about young children, a reality he had been happy to ignore while picking on her shortcomings. And, worse still, Antonio was still as prejudiced against her as he had been at their last meeting in Spain almost three years earlier...

Her memories of that period in her life were still surprisingly fresh and raw and her thoughts swept her back in time. Her sister's wedding had turned into a dream event for Sophie as well as the bride. Throughout that day, Antonio had smoothed Sophie's passage in a whole host of ways. He had complimented her on her appearance in the fussy purple dress that she had secretly absolutely detested. He had chatted to her while the photographs were being taken, arranged to have her sit near him at the reception and acted as interpreter and translator so that she could mix with the other guests. He had introduced her to lots of people, danced with her and acted as if her pleasure was his primary objective.

All that attention had been a very heady experience for Sophie, who would have felt vastly out of her depth in such smart company without Antonio's support. Her feet had barely touched the ground.

Belinda had been concerned enough to take Sophie aside to warn her off. 'Antonio's being very kind to you, but I don't want you to get the wrong idea about him—'

'I'm not getting *any* ideas about him,' Sophie protested in severe embarrassment, wondering if she had been making a fool of herself. After all, she had been doing all those despicable girlie things like batting her eyelashes at him and going for the giggle rather than the belly laugh.

'There's no way that Antonio would be attracted to you. Pablo says his brother's standards are so high that a saint couldn't make the grade with him,' her sister pointed out apologetically. 'But Antonio does have fantastic manners. Obviously he felt sorry for you when he found you on your own last night. I'm sure that's why he's making so much effort to ensure that you have a good time today.'

'Push off,' Sophie told Antonio when he next asked her to dance. 'When I need the sympathy vote, I'll let you know.'

'What are you talking about?' Antonio demanded with incredulity.

'I hear you're being kind to me because you took pity on me last night—'

'No, I'm really not that nice and unselfish.' His shimmering dark golden eyes connected with hers and held her entrapped. For the space of thirty seconds she was as out of touch with planet earth as a rocket powering into space. 'Was it your sister who told you that? I did notice her anxious looks. It's natural for her to want to protect you.'

Having driven her back to the apartment complex that night, he insisted on escorting her right into the shabby reception area. Once there, he quite casually suggested taking her out to eat the following evening and giving her a tour of a less busy part of the coast. Striving hard to match his cool, she accepted with a shrug and went into the lift with a light wave. Hopefully he hadn't noticed that she was so dizzy with excitement that she bumped her nose on the back wall of the lift.

Like Cinderella without the fairy godmother to help, Sophie toiled from dawn to dusk the next day striving to beautify herself for Antonio's benefit. Early that evening, however, her father and his girlfriend, Miriam split up. Miriam found Sophie's father with another woman and a huge argument took place. After listening wretchedly from the balcony to the fight that concluded in their separate departures, Sophie crept back indoors.

Ten minutes later Miriam's teenaged son, Terry, appeared. The boy was desperate to find his mother and prevent her from drowning her sorrows in drink. Only then did Sophie learn that Miriam was a recovering alcoholic. She was bitterly ashamed of her father's behaviour towards the poor woman. She also knew that she would not be able to live with her conscience if she did not help Terry look for his distraught parent.

Telling Antonio the full sordid truth of the goings-on at the apartment that day was not an option as far as

Sophie was concerned. It broke her heart to phone him and cancel their night out with the polite fiction that she had taken ill. He made no mention of an alternative arrangement and time was running out fast, for her flight home was only twenty-four hours away.

That search for Miriam through all the many bars in the resort was long and unsuccessful. Footsore, exhausted and too broke to afford a taxi, Sophie and Terry walked home by the beach in the early hours of the morning. Her heart leapt with joy when Antonio stepped out of a car parked across the street from the entrance. She told Terry to go on up to bed.

'I was so scared that I wasn't going to see you again,' she confided, too delighted by his appearance even to remember that she had pleaded sickness as an excuse for not seeing him earlier.

'You won't see me again.' Lean bronzed face hard, Antonio raked contemptuous dark-as-jet eyes over her.

Bewildered, she stared up at him, suddenly horribly conscious that she was looking even less glam than usual. 'But…but you're here now—why not?'

'How many reasons do you need? That you pretend to be ill when there's nothing wrong with you?'

'There was a reason for that—'

'*Sí.* I saw you with your arm round the young man in the Union Jack shirt. You've been on the beach with him,' Antonio murmured with mesmerising sibilance, letting a brown forefinger casually flick a stain on her vest top. 'And rolling in sand. I don't have to be a detective to know that you've been screwing outdoors.'

An argumentative drunk on the beach had kicked wet sand at her and soiled her white top and shorts. 'No, you've got it wrong—'

'*De veras?* I'm not into liars or tattoos.' Antonio angled a brief look of derision at the tiny colourful butterfly etched into the skin of her bare shoulder before concluding with succinct bite, 'Or for that matter, sluts.'

Sophie did not like to recall that she had been so keen on him that even after that rejection she had tried to contact him by phone to plead her innocence. Her initial calls had been unsuccessful and then he had phoned her to dismiss the whole situation with galling casualness.

'Stop worrying about this,' Antonio advised with nonchalant cool. 'There is no need for you to make any explanations to me. I had no right to criticise your behaviour. You went out on a date and told me a little white lie. It was nothing and now that we are related by marriage, even less than nothing.'

She discovered that his good manners could be the unyielding equivalent of an immoveable stone wall. He was equally firm about wishing her a good trip home and ending that brief conversation. It was a very long time before Sophie recovered from that disappointment. Foolish though it was, she had fallen madly in love within the space of forty-eight hours. So many times after that she wished that she had never laid eyes on Antonio Rocha. What she had never known she could not have missed. Nor would she have found herself pointlessly comparing the rough-and-ready males she met with a high-born Spanish noble.

Drifting back to the present, Sophie rediscovered her sense of purpose and hope. She was being too pessimistic. She had not really tried to reason with Antonio. Why should he want to take on the burden of a baby? He was a single guy, for goodness' sake! When Lydia had begun crying, Antonio had been totally unnerved. All she had to do was convince Antonio that she was capable of giving Lydia a loving and secure home. Maybe she would have to find fancier accommodation to please him, but if he was willing to contribute even a small amount towards Lydia's upkeep that would be possible. Surely then a compromise could be reached?

Antonio had decided to breakfast in the public restaurant rather than in the isolation of his suite. He had just finished eating when the head waiter approached his secluded table to inform him that he had a visitor waiting to see him in the lounge.

A gaunt older woman with grey hair scrambled up to introduce herself as Norah Moore. 'You don't know me, but I've known Sophie for years,' she proclaimed nervously. 'I know it's early but I wanted the chance to have a private word with you before you saw Sophie again.'

Antonio extended his hand. 'Antonio Rocha. Please sit down. Would you like something to drink? Perhaps tea?'

'Sophie said you had lovely manners…she was right. I don't need tea…thanks,' Norah told him anxiously. 'I'm here because I'm worried about Sophie.'

'How may I help you?' Antonio enquired.

'Sophie's wonderful with Lydia and terribly fond of the kiddie. You mustn't try to part them.'

'I only want what is best for my niece,' Antonio fielded gently.

'Sophie and your niece are as close as any mother and child. There's also the fact that Lydia's own mother wanted her sister to keep her child for good. I was a witness to that being said by Belinda,' the older woman continued squarely. 'Were you aware of that?'

'No, I was not,' Antonio conceded.

'There's something else too,' Norah continued heavily. 'Something I don't want to tell you but I feel I should tell you for Sophie's sake.'

'I can be discreet.'

'Well, Sophie can't have children of her own. She had leukaemia when she was a kid and the treatment messed her up. Did you know about that?'

'No, I was not aware of it,' Antonio said flatly, his strong bone structure tightening, the pallor of shock spreading below his bronzed skin.

Indeed he felt almost sick at that revelation. He was appalled to think of how she must have suffered as a child. He also knew how much Sophie would have loathed his knowledge of such a very personal matter. He did not question how he knew that. He was both angry and relieved that the older woman had decided to betray Sophie's confidence. His ignorance of just how vulnerable Sophie was had made him behave like a cruel bastard.

'So obviously that baby is very precious to Sophie. She's had a rotten life, you know,' Norah Moore continued accusingly. 'She works her fingers to the bone seven days a week trying to give that baby something better than she had herself. It may not look like much on your terms, but don't underestimate the sacrifices she's made. She looked after that daft sister of hers as well—'

'You have made your point, Mrs Moore.'

Having escorted the older woman out to her car, Antonio strode back into the hotel. What had Sophie said? *I honestly think I will die if you take her away from me.* He had preferred to be cynical about the depth of her affection for the child. Now, and thanks only to a stranger's intervention, he was being forced to face the probability that Sophie was very deeply attached to the child and with good reason if she could not have a baby of her own. He was dealing with a much more complex situation than he had appreciated. If he was to deprive Sophie of Lydia, might grief drive her into doing something foolish? He breathed in slow and deep and then out again in a measured hiss of acceptance. That was not a risk he felt it would be reasonable for him to take. For the first time he acknowledged that Lydia was as much Sophie's niece as his.

CHAPTER FOUR

LATER that morning, Sophie saw the limousine first. Antonio swung out and unfolded to his full intimidating height and she had eyes only for him. Immaculate in appearance and stunningly handsome, he was wearing a formal charcoal-grey suit teamed with a white shirt and a blue silk tie. Dragging her enthralled attention from him, she smoothed damp palms down over her most presentable T-shirt.

She was so nervous she started talking before she even had the door properly open. 'A friend is looking after Lydia for me…I thought we could talk on the beach… It's a lovely day.'

Lovely? Antonio thought the sky was cloudy, the wind rather strong and the temperature distinctly on the cool side. But then even at its best the British climate could not compete with the sun-drenched heat of his own country, he conceded ruefully.

'We would have more privacy indoors,' he suggested.

Sophie tensed. 'I don't want you to see where I live,' she admitted.

Antonio raised a bemused brow. '*Por qué*…why?'

Sophie began walking along the path that led down to the strand. 'After that crack you made about poverty, I just wouldn't feel comfortable entertaining you in my home. It may not be much but I like it. Why should I have to put up with you acting like I'm living in a hovel?'

'I hope I would not be so rude,' Antonio drawled flatly.

'Well, you were yesterday,' Sophie could not resist telling him. 'On the beach, we'll be equal.'

Antonio was not dressed for the beach. He wondered if that was supposed to be part of the great levelling exercise or if she was secretly hoping that he would freak out when he got sand on his shoes. He watched her race to the edge of the water like an eager child, her every movement fired with mercurial energy. Beautiful to look at, but almost impossible to handle. She was unpredictable, hot-tempered, impulsive, wildly emotional: she was driving him mad. The proposition he was about to outline, however, would restore the status quo. She would become much more amenable to his guidance when she was living in Spain…

'I've worked out a compromise since we talked last night,' Antonio imparted in his smooth honeyed drawl.

'Oh…?' Her spirits lifted by the bright reflection of the sun on the sea, Sophie pinned hopeful eyes to his bold bronzed profile.

'You can move to Spain.'

'No way!' Sophie gasped in disconcertion.

'Try not to interrupt me.' Dark golden eyes levelled on her mutinous face. 'Lydia will have to live at the *castillo* with me, but I own many properties nearby. Finding you accommodation would not be a problem and it would be free. You could see the child whenever you liked and she would find it easier to adapt to her new home if you were there to provide support.'

Sophie folded her arms with a jerk. She could not believe his nerve. 'So I give up my life here, move abroad and live in limbo on your property like some charity case. Thanks, but no, thanks! I'm not unreasonable. I'm happy to share Lydia with you but I refuse to hand her over to you lock, stock, and barrel. I mean, what are you planning to do with her?'

'Engage childcare professionals to take care of her every need.'

Her green eyes flamed. 'That really says it all, doesn't it? Why can't you just be honest? You haven't the slightest personal interest in your brother's child. You think it's your duty to give her a home, but you resent it—'

'That is not true.' But there was enough of a grain of truth in that accusation to flick Antonio on the raw.

'You'll never love Lydia the way I do because you're always going to see her as a burden!'

'You're wrong,' Antonio incised almost fiercely.

'Of course you will. She's not your baby and you didn't ask for her and you're not that fussed about kids anyway…and if you get married Lydia's likely to be as popular as rat poison with your wife!'

'I have no intention of getting married—'

Adrenalin pounding through her veins, Sophie stalked over to him to look up at him, her eyes bright with conviction. 'But she needs a mother, Antonio. Not people you pay to wash and feed her.'

'I'm not ready for marriage.'

'Then let Lydia and I alone and send us the occasional postcard!' Sophie advised thinly, her temper rising at her inability to gain an emotional reaction from him. 'You're too selfish to take charge of a baby. You'll neglect her. You'll be too busy wheeling and dealing at the office and socialising with your harem of women to make time for her!'

Brilliant eyes shimmering into a hot golden blaze, Antonio closed long fingers round Sophie's wrist to urge her closer. 'Harem?' he prompted with subdued mockery.

Angry, mortified colour burnished Sophie's cheeks. 'Pablo used to tell Belinda all about your exploits with your string of women.'

'Pablo would have known nothing. We were not close. I did not confide in him. But while I may not talk of my conquests I'm not ashamed of my sex life. Did you think I would be?' Arrogant dark head high, Antonio gazed down at her, lush black lashes semi-screening his disturbingly intent gaze.

'I don't give two hoots about your flippin' sex life!' Sophie flung in affronted denial, her cheeks burning.

'I think you do…' Antonio breathed soft and low, the dark timbre of his deep, rich drawl feathering down her slender spine like a hurricane warning. 'I think that nearly three years ago I was too much of a gentleman for your tastes—'

'Gentleman is not a word I would label you with,' Sophie cut in unevenly, a hunger she could not suppress licking up in her pelvis and freezing her where she stood bare inches from him. Every inch of her was taut and screaming with so powerful an awareness of her own body that she felt light-headed. All she needed from him was one kiss, she was telling herself. One kiss just to see what all the fuss was about and she was convinced that he would be as much of a disappointment as every other guy she had kissed. But in Antonio's case, it would be a glorious, wonderful disappointment that would for ever banish her unease around him.

'But, whatever the label, you're still hot for me, *mi cielo*,' Antonio murmured huskily.

Sophie trembled. 'Curious…' she admitted in a breath of sound, her throat dry and tight.

Antonio never kissed women in public. He gazed down at her, his attention welded to the darkened emerald of her expectant eyes and the ruby allure of her luscious, parted lips. He lifted a hand to close his fingers into her curls, learning that her hair felt soft as silk and picturing the rebellious golden-toffee waves spread across his pillows. Thought had nothing to do with what happened next.

His mouth touched hers; she stopped breathing. He brushed her lips light as a butterfly and then slowly deepened the pressure. She was torn by delight and impatience and a mortifying desire to grab him with both hands. Tantalised beyond bearing, she leant towards him, wildly conscious of the aching heaviness of her breasts below her T-shirt, the swelling sensitivity of the rosy crowns abraded by the rough cotton. She knew she wanted his mouth there too and the very thought shocked her rigid, but she could no more pull back from him and temptation than she could have stemmed the tide.

'Antonio…' she whispered.

'I don't want this…' Antonio growled, but he went back for more of it all the same.

Passion banished restraint as he used his tongue to delve deep into the moist interior of her mouth. That invasive tactic had the most extraordinary effect on Sophie. The taste and feel of him drove her wild. An excitement close to the edge of pain shot like flame through her slender length. She shivered violently and locked her arms round his neck, kissing him back with unconditional fervour. The heat and strength of his lean, powerful body hard against her softer curves left her breathless and gasping.

In an abrupt movement, Antonio wrenched himself back from her. Stunning eyes a scorching gold, he was breathing heavily. For a split second, Sophie was lost in a time slip, still craving that intoxicating tide of sensation. Then self-preservation kicked in and she spun away, digging shaking hands into the pockets of her jeans and dragging in oxygen in a greedy gulp. He was dynamite. She hadn't wanted to find that out. But equally quickly it dawned on her that the attraction was not one-sided, as she had once naïvely believed.

Her body felt electrified and deprived, but her mind was racing. A wicked sense of triumph put her embarrassment to flight. Antonio Rocha, Marqués de Salazar might think that he was vastly superior to her in every way, but he still fancied her. Whoopee! Yay! She was tempted to dance round the beach and sing. In one fell swoop, in the space of one revealing kiss, almost three years of believing that she had made an outsize fool of herself in Spain had been wiped out. Antonio was more into tattoos than he was ever likely to admit.

The silence stretched like an endless cavern where light never shone.

Feeling indecently smug and ashamed of herself, Sophie veiled her sparkling eyes and reflected dizzily that she had never imagined a kiss could be that volatile.

'We were talking about you taking up residence in Spain,' Antonio reminded her drily.

He sounded so cool and calm that her buoyant mood deflated as if he had stuck a pin in her. All right, maybe he was only a teensy weensy bit attracted to her. It took enormous effort for her to recapture her ability to concentrate. 'Spain…that idea's not on,' she countered in a flat undertone. 'We'd be in your country and Lydia would be in your home and I wouldn't have any rights. You would be making all the decisions about her. You could easily change your mind about allowing me to see her—'

'You would have to trust me.'

'I don't,' Sophie confided without hesitation. 'I'd have too much to lose. And I just know you'll get married and that would change everything—'

'I am not about to get married. What is this obsession?'

Sophie was unimpressed. She shot him a sidelong glance. Her heartbeat speeded up. He really was breathtakingly handsome. 'Now or five years from now, what difference would it make to me? I'd still be powerless and no wife of yours is likely to allow me to stick my oar in where Lydia's concerned. Your wife would have far more say in her upbringing than I would ever have—'

'*Por favor Dios*... I enjoy my freedom. I won't take a wife for at least ten years!'

'I just want to be with Lydia. That's *all* that I want,' Sophie stressed with pained dignity. 'I love her...you don't. I mean...maybe you're always going to look at her and remember your brother. Don't tell me that he was your favourite person!'

His strong jaw line squared at that inflammatory statement. But he was no hypocrite. As she spun away to hide the tears burning her eyes he tugged her back round to face him, his every move redolent of the confidence that powered him. 'Come back to my hotel with me for lunch...'

Suddenly shy of him again, terrifyingly sensitive to

the intimate tone of his accented voice, Sophie coloured. 'You're not thinking of food.'

Antonio gave her a hard, devastating smile that was quite unrepentant. 'You're so direct—'

His lack of self-consciousness infuriated her and her whole face stiffened. 'I imagine I'd disappoint you.'

'I don't think so.' His stunning dark, deep-set eyes flared reflective gold.

'Purely as a point of speculation, how much would you give up to be with Lydia all the time?'

Her smooth brow pleated. 'I'd do anything for that.'

The silence eddied around her like a dangerous current.

Antonio surveyed her without expression. 'If you had constant access to Lydia and security, would you be prepared to do everything I asked in return for that privilege?'

'Short of crime, yes,' she agreed urgently, but her bewilderment was growing. 'Why are you asking me that?'

'If Lydia needs a mother twenty-four seven, then I should marry. But I like my life as it is. That's the problem,' Antonio admitted with a candour he had never employed with a woman before.

'That you don't want a wife?'

'If I opted for a marriage of convenience instead the problem would vanish. That kind of marriage might last between five and ten years max before ending in an amicable divorce.'

Sophie was hanging on his every word but she was totally confused. 'Why are you telling me this?'

'I think there's a possibility that we could reach a mutually beneficial agreement,' Antonio murmured thoughtfully. 'The wife I choose would have to know the score. I would expect to retain my freedom to come and go as and when I liked and with whom I pleased.'

'You're talking about a fake marriage?' Sophie pressed uncertainly. 'Are you suggesting that you and me—?'

'You would gain Lydia and financial security and my life would continue as normal. That would be the deal.'

Green eyes huge, she stared up at him, transfixed by the concept of marrying him. 'The deal? *But*—'

'You'd be insane to turn me down,' Antonio asserted, examining the arrangement from every angle and more and more impressed by his own creative ingenuity.

He believed that it was as close to perfect as a solution could be. Even so it would only be a temporary solution and he would have to have a watertight prenuptial contract drawn up. Sophie, however, would have no illusions as to the nature of their agreement. She would make her home on his country estate and take full charge of their niece and his conscience could be easy. As soon as he had learned that Sophie was infertile, he had known that it would be indescribably cruel to deprive her of Lydia. But only by marrying Sophie would he be able to watch over the child's interests without being unduly troubled by further responsibility.

His grandmother, however, might well be aghast when Sophie, with her poor background and education, became his bride, but Doña Ernesta was a strong woman and she would get over her disappointment. The rest of the family and his friends would be shocked as well. Always an individual, he decided he could live with that. In any case he was finally willing to recall just how many people had been charmed by Sophie's vivacity when they had met her in Spain. Doña Ernesta would very probably take charge of her and teach her anything she needed to know. His grandparent would also benefit from having full access to Pablo's daughter without the burden of having to worry about the quality of the child's care.

Sophie stared up at Antonio in unconcealed wonderment. He was asking her to marry him so that he could offer her a home with Lydia in Spain. It certainly would be a marriage of convenience, she thought breathlessly, for she could not imagine two people with less in common. Yet it was also a very practical answer to the problem of Lydia's future welfare. Even so, she was still amazed that he should be willing to marry her for Lydia's sake and that he should have come up with that idea quite so quickly.

'*Dios mio!* Say yes and let's get off the beach,' Antonio urged with masculine impatience.

Sophie blinked. 'You can't just throw something like that at me and expect—?'

Antonio dealt her a bold look of challenge. 'Why shouldn't I expect an immediate positive response? You're cleaning floors to put food on the table. You live in a home with wheels under it and it's so shabby you won't let me see it. I have offered you a ticket out of hell.'

Sophie reddened and shifted worriedly off one foot onto the other. 'It's not that simple…this isn't hell—'

In the cool breeze, Antonio suppressed a shiver: he was freezing. He looked out at the grey sea under the grey sky and then down at the even duller shingle below his feet. 'It *is* by my standards.'

'But you're rich and spoilt—'

'Wouldn't you like to be rich and spoilt too?' Antonio murmured smooth as silk, planting a lean brown hand to her narrow back to gently press her back towards the path.

'I can't imagine being rich...but I think I'd like being spoilt,' Sophie confided tightly. 'Is this a joke? Or are you serious?'

'If you can accept a marriage that has a finish date in sight and a husband who is a free agent, I'm serious.'

A husband who was a free agent was a contradiction in terms, Sophie reflected abstractedly. Her head was buzzing with too many thoughts at once. She was astonished, fearful, excited, distrustful and confused all at one and the same time. But she had not been exaggerating when she had said that there was nothing she would not do to be with Lydia.

Marry Antonio? Learn how to be a demure wife? Overlook his infidelity? Her gut reactions warned her that that was wrong and absolutely against her own principles. But then she reminded herself that Antonio was not suggesting a normal marriage. She could scarcely apply the usual moral standards to an arrangement that he had referred to as a 'deal.' A wholly self-centred deal calculated to cause the least possible interference with his enjoyment of his life, she conceded ruefully. But how could she blame him for that? His lack of interest in being a proper parent to Lydia was the only reason he was willing to make it possible for Sophie to continue filling that role for their niece's benefit.

'You have until tonight to decide your answer. I'll send the limo to pick you up and bring you back to my hotel for dinner.' Having reached the top of the path, Antonio was already signalling his chauffeur to indicate his readiness to depart.

Sophie could not help recalling the heady few minutes on the beach when Antonio had awarded her his full attention. That kiss had rocked her world. Now his spectacular dark golden eyes were cool and distant again. His indifference was a slap in the face, a rejection as much as an acknowledgement that their kiss had not been equally special on his terms. In comparison, Sophie was all too well aware that for her the kiss had been seriously addictive stuff. Just thinking about that wicked blaze of excitement made her feel incredibly hot and quivery and very unwilling to look at him.

'What time?' she asked, striving to match his cool with her own.

'Eight.'

'I don't have anything fancy to wear,' she warned him.

'It's not a problem. We'll dine in my suite.'

Sophie got the message. Unless she could present what he deemed to be an acceptable image, she would not be seen in public. Or was she being over-sensitive? Even a little unfair? After all, she would have Lydia with her, and if the baby became sleepy Antonio's suite would be quieter than a public restaurant. She watched him smile, spring into his opulent limousine and depart. It was the sort of throwaway smile he might have given anybody. She was conscious of a deep-seated need to see him smile and know it was just for her.

That evening, and only half an hour late—which was really good going for Sophie in terms of promptness—she travelled up in the lift to Antonio's suite. She had Lydia cradled by one arm on her hip. 'Now remember…lots of smiles. You've got to make the running with Antonio and sell yourself,' she instructed the baby gazing up at her with trusting brown eyes. 'He's sensitive to screams, so you have to take the fear out of fathering for him. If you cry again, he's going to avoid you like the plague…okay?'

A middle-aged guy dressed like a waiter ushered her into the suite.

'Is Antonio in?' Sophie asked nervously and the man responded in what might have been Spanish with an apologetic shake of his head.

She hovered in the centre of the fabulous reception room, shook her head when a sofa was indicated and did so again when the drinks cabinet was spread invitingly wide. A communicating door opened and Antonio appeared. Relief and tension struggled inside her. 'I thought maybe you were out.'

In one skimming glance Antonio took in the unexpected presence of the baby and settled his attention on Sophie. In a shabby cord jacket with a fur-trimmed hood and black trousers ornamented with an embarrassment of zips, she looked painfully young. Her sudden vivacious smile lit up her heart-shaped face and for a split second he forgot what he was about to say and simply stared.

'I'm sorry I wasn't available when you arrived,' Antonio responded, his recovery almost immediate while on another level he sought to solve the riddle of her appeal. 'I was taking a call. Did Maureo offer you a drink?'

'Is that his name? I didn't want anything. It's nice of you not to say anything about me being late.'

'I have a great respect for punctuality,' Antonio sliced back softly.

'We're going to have a problem,' Sophie forecast with unblemished good humour. 'I try really hard to be on time, but things tend to hold me up. Everywhere I go I'm always running against the clock—'

'Better organisation will improve that.'

Sophie wondered if he had any idea how hard it was to organise a baby.

'Maureo would like to take your coat,' Antonio explained as the older man hovered nearby.

'Would you like to hold Lydia?' Sophie asked brightly, ignoring the tautening of his spectacular bone structure and moving closer to helpfully tug up his arm and pass her niece deftly into his grasp. 'Smile and talk to her…she loves people.'

Antonio marvelled at how little Lydia seemed to weigh. He could not recall ever taking a close look at a baby before. With her soft fluff of curls, creamy skin and big brown eyes, she was really quite pretty, he decided in surprise. He could see no resemblance to Pablo. His mobile phone rang. The baby jerked, her face screwing up as she loosed a plaintive howl of fright. Antonio stuffed Lydia back into Sophie's arms with unconcealed haste.

'*Perdón…*' He took his call.

Sophie soothed Lydia and interpreted Maureo's gestures to take a seat at the table by the window. Antonio was talking in a foreign language, moving his hands to accentuate certain points with a confidence that she found irresistibly attractive. His lean, darkly handsome features were intent with concentration. Some day, Sophie thought fiercely, I want him to look at me like that. Like I'm important and interesting. In shock at that lowering aspiration that had come out of nowhere at her, she froze. Shame-faced, she cleared her mind and refused to think about it again. She would marry Antonio because that was the price of keeping Lydia. That, she assured herself firmly, was the only reason she had for marrying him. Only a real idiot would get romantic ideas about a guy who said he wanted to be a free agent.

Maureo reappeared toting a highchair for Lydia. Thanking him warmly, she strapped her niece in and put some toys on the tray to keep her occupied.

'You're a very busy guy,' Sophie remarked brittlely when Antonio sat down opposite and the first course had arrived.

'Invariably.'

'Well, like you forecast, I'm about to say yes to the deal. But I have a couple of conditions to make,' Sophie told him while she opened the small container she had brought with her, put some finger foods on her side plate and set them down in front of Lydia.

'Conditions?'

'I want to have a proper wedding,' Sophie advanced uncomfortably. 'Nothing fancy, just us and the witnesses with a few frills…a dress and some photos to make us look like a *real* couple. I don't want Lydia to know this is a deal and not an ordinary marriage.'

'She's six months old,' Antonio murmured drily.

'But she won't always be. I don't ever want her to know that I had to marry you to keep her because that would make her feel bad—'

'Why should it?'

'I remember how I felt knowing I was just a burden to the grown-ups who looked after me.' Sophie set a feeding cup down on the tray of the highchair, her delicate profile taut. 'So, what do you think?'

Antonio recognised that he had not thought through every angle. He had no plans to go public with an announcement that he was making a marriage of convenience. Consequently, he would have no choice but to act out a charade of normality. Appearances mattered little to him, but to the majority of his family appearances were everything. 'The frills aren't a problem but I would like the wedding to be quiet and discreet. What other conditions?'

Sophie worried at her full lower lip with her teeth before speaking. 'Just one… I want you to promise me that you'll try to be a father to Lydia.'

Antonio flung back his arrogant dark head and dealt her a searing look of indignation. 'Who are you to address me on such a subject?'

Sophie was very pale but she persisted. 'This is just a deal for you. You've made that clear. But you're still likely to be the only father Lydia ever has.'

'The deal is between you and I only. My niece's position in my life is unassailable,' Antonio spelt out with cold clarity. 'I will naturally make every effort to fulfil a paternal role.'

The main course arrived in the tense silence that followed.

'I will not apologise. You were offensive,' Antonio drawled when Maureo had departed again.

Watching Antonio look challenged as Lydia grizzled because she was over tired, Sophie tried not to wonder when his parenting efforts would begin.

'I have certain conditions too,' Antonio affirmed. 'Before the wedding can take place you will have to sign a pre-nuptial agreement.'

Unexpectedly Sophie grinned. 'Like a Hollywood star?' she prompted in visible excitement. 'Are you really that rich? Crazy!'

'The agreement will specify financial arrangements and—'

'Yeah, yeah, yeah… Do we have to talk about that now?' Lifting Lydia down onto her lap to soothe her fractious whimpers, Sophie ate her meal with a fork in one hand, quite unconscious of Antonio's amazement at her dexterity. He watched his niece's eyes drift shut in contentment and marvelled at Sophie's remarkable control over a baby whom he considered to be as volatile as dynamite. He congratulated himself on having made a very wise decision: Sophie was worth five nannies.

'We can leave any discussion of the terms of the pre-nup to our lawyers.'

'I don't have any—'

'You must engage one for independent advice.'

Sophie wasn't listening. She gazed across the table at Antonio, dazzled by the stunning symmetry of his lean bronzed face, and her eyes took on a dreamy cast. 'What do you want me to wear for the wedding?' she asked softly.

'I have no wish to be rude,' Antonio confided silkily, 'but why should I have an opinion on what you might wear?'

The mental soap bubble in which Sophie was floating her make-believe world burst with a bang that hurt and humiliated. Her face went pink and hot.

'You blush like a schoolgirl,' Antonio mocked.

'Fancy that!' she tossed back and pushed away her plate, all appetite ebbing.

Sophie was really annoyed with herself for that brief flight of foolishness. If Antonio had decided he needed to deliver a reality check, she could hardly blame him. After all, why *would* he be interested in how she dressed for their fake wedding? Why had she even asked that stupid, stupid question?

'So, apart from what's already been agreed, what are the rules of this deal?' Sophie enquired briskly.

'Mutual respect and cooperation, *querida.*' Antonio signalled Maureo and the wineglasses were topped up for a toast.

Sophie interpreted his objective without difficulty. She might fancy Antonio Rocha rotten, but at his most basic she understood his expectations as clearly as if he had voiced them: she was to respect him and strive unceasingly to fit in with all his wishes, reasonable and otherwise. He was noble, he was rich and he was successful and she was poor and illegitimate and lived in a home with wheels under it. Equality could not exist in such diversity. Antonio exuded the proud benevolence of a male convinced he was making a hugely generous sacrifice for which she ought to be undyingly grateful.

Soft, full mouth set mutinously taut, Sophie dropped a kiss down onto Lydia's little drooping head and rejoiced in the baby's soft, trusting weight against her. Her pride might be stinging, but she had to be more sensible and less sensitive, she scolded herself. If Antonio ensured that she and Lydia had a comfortable home and a secure future, he *did* deserve her gratitude.

CHAPTER FIVE

'VERY colourful...very unusual,' Norah finally selected with obvious difficulty.

It was Sophie's wedding day and, as she fully expected that it would be the only wedding day she ever had, she was keen to make the most of the occasion. Refusing to be deflated by the older woman's lack of enthusiasm, Sophie twirled yet again just for the fun of seeing her dress flounce round slim legs enhanced by perilously high pink diamanté-trimmed shoes. She was overwhelmed by the pleasure of wearing the latest fashion for the first time in her life. Although she adored clothes she had never had the money to follow design trends. Determined not to pose as a conventional bride and run the risk of awakening Antonio's derision, Sophie had decided to be more audacious in her choice of outfit. She was even more proud of having used only a tiny bit of the money in the bank account that he had insisted on opening on her behalf.

It was three weeks since she had dined at Antonio's hotel and three weeks since she had seen him. Norah Moore had made no secret of her concern over Sophie's decision to marry Lydia's uncle and even though the ceremony was due to take place in less than an hour she still could not hide her disquiet.

'Please cheer up and be happy for Lydia and me,' Sophie begged.

'But you shouldn't be marrying Antonio for Lydia's

benefit,' Norah muttered uncomfortably. 'I'm afraid I never imagined *this* happening.'

'Who did?' Sophie asked breezily. 'But if I have to share Lydia with Antonio, this is the best way to go about it. He wouldn't let me bring her up here on my own. And how could I have moved to Spain and coped with just being a visitor in her life?'

'But perhaps leaving your options open that way would have been more sensible at first. From what you've said about Antonio...well,' Norah continued awkwardly, her worn face rather stiff, 'he sounds like a trustworthy man—'

'Don't put those two words together. I wouldn't trust Antonio out of my sight.'

'You can't judge all men by your father's example.'

Sophie shrugged. 'Antonio doesn't owe me any favours, so I had to be suspicious of his motives. I also have to look out for Lydia—'

'It's still not too late to call this wedding off. I don't feel that it's right for you to marry Antonio Rocha.'

Amazed by the older woman's persistence on that score, Sophie frowned in bewilderment. 'Why not? Antonio knows exactly what he's doing. I bet he divorces me even faster than he said he would and shunts Lydia and I off to live somewhere well out of his way. He doesn't care about Lydia the way I do—'

'He hasn't had the chance or the time. A lot of men feel uncomfortable around babies—'

'Why are you so against me marrying him?'

Norah flushed and turned away, her discomfiture unconcealed. Sophie reckoned she knew why, but she was too fond of the other woman to hurt her feelings by being too blunt. Understandably, Norah did not want her to move to Spain. Sophie also suspected that Norah had secretly hoped that Sophie might eventually have a change of heart and start dating her son, Matt. Even though she had never given Matt the slightest encouragement, Sophie had always felt rather guilty about him. His stoic air of misery as the wedding day drew closer had made her feel worse.

'I just thought there might be some other way of bringing up Lydia other than marrying the marqués,' Norah muttered evasively.

'This way Lydia will find out about the Spanish side of her family and learn how to be really exclusive and up-market like…well, like some rich kid,' Sophie pointed out. 'She's going to pick up all sorts of stuff I could never teach her. It's what Belinda would have wanted for her—'

'Yes, it probably is.' Norah nodded thoughtfully. 'Your sister did set great store by that sort of thing. I shouldn't have kept on nagging at you. I can see that belonging to a rich family like Antonio's will give Lydia a terrific start in life and opportunities that she would never get here.'

'She deserves the best.' Sophie was grateful that the older woman was finally thinking along the same lines and accepting her reasons for marrying Antonio. 'That's the only reason I'm doing this…for *her*.'

Forty minutes later, Sophie studied the crowd of people waiting outside the church with some surprise. Had a previous wedding started late and overrun its time? Oh, dear, she thought, Antonio would not like that. Well, they would just have to wait their turn. She checked her reflection to see that the tiny concoction of pink chiffon and feathers perched on top of her curls was still at the right angle. She smoothed nervous hands down over the fitted skirt of her dress, which was made of an exuberant fabric covered with big splashy roses. The limo driver pulled in right at the church steps and jumped out to open the door.

With Lydia in a carrier seat, Sophie climbed out. Noisy people shouting piercing questions and waving cameras surrounded her.

'What's your name?' someone asked.

'Friend of the bride's?' someone else shouted from the back.

'She's not a guest, she *is* the bride!' Norah proclaimed sternly. 'Now move and let us inside the church…we've got a baby here!'

'Are you Sophie Cunningham?' a voice demanded in astonishment.

Momentarily transfixed as she was by the sound of her name on a stranger's lips, a nervous giggle escaped Sophie. Taking advantage of the gap that had appeared in the crush as Lydia's presence was acknowledged, she hurried on up the steps and into the porch. The elderly priest greeted her warmly.

Norah took charge of Lydia. Sophie's heart started beating very fast. She sucked in a steadying breath and took a peek down the aisle. Sunlight was pouring through the stained-glass windows and bathing the interior in beautiful jewelled streamers of rich colour. Antonio was at the altar, another smaller, slighter man standing to one side of him, probably the lawyer he had mentioned. She was more interested in staring at Antonio. Even in profile, he looked incredibly handsome. His formal dark suit and white shirt were exquisitely tailored to his tall, powerful frame. As usual he exuded the quiet, distinguished elegance that seemed so much a part of him.

When she drew level with him, she wanted so badly

for him to acknowledge her arrival with a look, a smile, the merest touch, but nothing happened. He had phoned her several times over the past three weeks but the calls had been brief and businesslike. As the nuptial mass began she listened carefully to every word. Each of them made their responses, her voice uneven with a sense of the gravity of the occasion, his cool and firm. He slid a gold ring on her finger without betraying a hint of proper masculine hesitance.

Only with the greatest difficulty was Antonio restraining his ire. The paparazzi were encamped outside. The discreet event he had had organised had been blown wide open. His family avoided publicity like the plague. Who had talked? One of his own staff? A hotel employee? Someone attached to the church? Or his bride? He had expected Sophie to show up in a very frilly over-the-top long white dress complete with veil. In a funny sort of way that he was reluctant to analyse, he had been rather looking forward to seeing her in a wedding gown. Instead she was sporting the most extraordinarily inappropriate apparel. Her outrageously floral dress was flashy enough to stop rush-hour traffic. He studied her ridiculously tiny perky hat. He knew he was being punished for not giving her the advice she had asked for: it was his own fault.

'Stop right there…' Norah instructed, holding up her camera as the bride and groom turned away from the altar.

Antonio looked down into Sophie's misty green eyes fringed by curling dark lashes. Her soft pink mouth was the same shade as the hat and it was amazing how well that particular colour became her, Antonio reflected grudgingly.

'Sorry about this…but there's times when you have

to bite the bullet and just do what you have to do,' Sophie whispered apologetically, gripping hold of his arms to stretch herself up to him. 'Act like you're going to kiss me…this one's for the album I'm going to make for Lydia.'

Antonio closed long, lean fingers into the toffee-coloured curls tumbling down her spine, tugged her head back and brought his hungry mouth down hard on hers. In shock, she jerked against him and gasped as if she were being ravished. Even as pure lust leapt through him he wanted to laugh. It was time she accepted that he was a Rocha and like every Rocha right back to the sixteenth century: he didn't take orders; he handed them out.

His tongue delved deep in a bold invasion. A piercing, unbearable sweetness shot through Sophie followed by a fierce wave of heat. Dizzy, she locked her arms round his neck to stay upright, and as he released her tingling lips she struggled to catch her breath against his shoulder. He set her back from him in the thrumming silence. Norah was staring wide-eyed. Crimson with embarrassment, Sophie stared into space, her mind blanked out by shock at her own wanton behaviour.

Impervious to that kind of discomfiture, Antonio introduced her very briefly to the lawyer, who, having acted as their second witness, was already making his departure. The official photographer, whose services had been arranged, awaited them in the church porch. At Antonio's request he produced his driving licence as proof of his identity.

'I'm sorry but the presence of the journalists outside means that a photographic session will not be possible,' Antonio imparted gravely. 'That will not, of course, make any difference to your remuneration.'

Emerging from her fog of self-loathing over that kiss, Sophie exclaimed, 'But you can't cancel the photographs!'

'I can do whatever I like, *mi rica.*' His quiet tone audible only to her ears, Antonio gazed down at her with grim dark eyes. 'If you're responsible for that rabble of reporters out there, you're likely to be very disappointed by the coverage they gain of our wedding. We're leaving now by the rear exit.'

'Those people are newspaper reporters?' Sophie was bewildered by his speech. 'Why are you suggesting that I might have something to do with them being here?'

'We'll discuss that later,' Antonio informed her at a pitch that would have frozen volcanic lava in its tracks.

Sophie thought that perhaps she had misunderstood what he had said and returned to her main source of concern. 'You *can't* just cancel the photos!'

'Might I suggest,' the photographer dared in a deferential murmur, 'That a change of location would suffice?'

Considerably more interested in heading direct to the airport and his flight home to Spain and normality, Antonio set his even white teeth together at that unwelcome suggestion.

'Look,' Sophie said urgently, 'Let me go out and tell those reporters to get lost!'

Seriously taken aback by that suggestion, Antonio studied his bride. She might be five feet nothing in height, but there was a definite suggestion of belligerence in her irate stance. She was confrontational and naïve. He had a disturbing image of the headlines that would erupt if his wife waded in to exchange insults with a posse of paparazzi. It began to dawn on him for the first time that being married to Sophie might not be the equivalent of a walk in the park. It was a sobering reflection for a male who had intended to safeguard his freedom by taking a wife.

'You can't let them ruin the day,' Sophie protested at his elbow. 'That would be like giving way to blackmail.'

Antonio stifled a derisive desire to admit that all of a sudden he knew exactly how that felt. 'We'll use the grounds of the hotel.'

His reward for that peace-keeping concession was immediate and startling. Sophie flung both arms round him and gave him an enthusiastic hug. 'Thanks. *Thanks!* You won't regret it.'

Before the bridal couple left the building, however, Norah Moore also insisted on taking her leave of them. 'No, I'm not coming one step further to play gooseberry,' she responded wryly when Sophie took her off to one side in an effort to persuade her to accompany them to the hotel. 'You should just have said that you and Antonio…well, that kiss said it all for you, didn't it? I didn't know where to look!'

Reminded of what an exhibition she had made of herself, Sophie squirmed in shame and chagrin. 'It wasn't like you think.'

'It was just as it should be. Your getting married will be good for my Matt too,' the older woman informed her bluntly. 'He's been trailing after you like a lovelorn puppy, but now he'll have to get over you.'

In the limo on the way to the hotel, Sophie turned to Antonio and said, 'Why did you suggest that I might be responsible for all those journalists turning up at the church?'

Stunning dark eyes unflinching, he looked levelly back at her. 'Someone tipped them off.'

'Not me…for goodness' sake, I didn't even know the newspapers would be interested in what you get up to!'

Antonio said nothing.

Her temper roused, Sophie watched him from below her lashes. 'Aren't you going to apologise?'

'If I misjudged you, I'm sorry—'

'If?' Sophie was outraged by the wording he had chosen to use.

'I don't yet know who's responsible for alerting the paparazzi,' Antonio countered silkily, as immoveable as solid rock in his resolve not to yield the point.

'Well, it wasn't me and we're not going to have a very friendly relationship if you keep on accusing me of things I didn't do!' Sophie warned him in high dudgeon.

'Who said we have to be friendly?' Antonio drawled with deliberate provocation, lounging fluidly back in his corner of the limousine to enjoy the entertainment. He liked watching her vibrate with emotion, for that intense capacity for feeling was as rare in his experience as a genuine Stradivarius violin.

'But you just married me!' Sophie condemned furiously.

'Since when did matrimony and friendship go hand in hand?' Having made that statement to keep her simmering, Antonio surveyed her from below lush black lashes. Once again his analytical mind was engaged in attempting to dissect the mystery of her pulling power. It wasn't just her passion. Inexplicably that tiny hat anchored to her mane of curls now struck him as the very essence of femininity. His wide, sensual mouth compressed. In fact she looked amazingly sexy.

'That's a horrible thing to say!' Sophie condemned.

'I have a whole host of lifelong married ancestors who cohabited with hatred.'

'That doesn't surprise me one little bit!' Sophie slung back.

Antonio was now endeavouring to work out why she looked so sexy. He still thought the dress was a mistake, but it did somehow contrive to accentuate her delicate grace to perfection. The neckline revealed only a modest hint of shadowy cleavage. She had surprisingly full breasts for her slender build. Even overblown roses could not conceal that ripe, rounded swell from his attention. At that point and very much to his annoyance, his libido kicked in with almost painful enthusiasm. She shifted position, her hemline riding up to expose a slim length of thigh. A wolf to the slaughter, his gaze lingered to trace the limb's progression into a shapely knee and slender calf that concluded in amazingly narrow ankles and very small feet. Suddenly he wanted her under him with a ferocity that astonished him.

'Pablo was cruel to Belinda,' Sophie breathed abruptly. 'I just want you to know I won't put up with that kind of treatment!'

All desire stifled by that disquieting revelation, Antonio settled brilliant dark golden eyes on her. 'What did he do?'

'What didn't he do?' Sophie traded heavily with a slight shiver, her anger with Antonio ebbing while she remembered what her sister had told her. 'He killed her confidence. He was always criticising her and telling her how stupid she was and cutting her off in front of other people.'

'I am not my brother,' Antonio spelt out with measured clarity.

'Oh, I know that. Pablo wouldn't have cared what

happened to his niece. He would only have got involved if there was money in the offing,' Sophie ceded grudgingly.

She was not in the mood to say anything that Antonio might construe as a compliment. But there it was, whether she liked it or not—Antonio was a positive prince among men when set next to his late brother.

'I dislike being compared to Pablo,' Antonio informed her with cold emphasis.

Feeling snubbed for having been generous enough to point out that he was much more responsible and caring, Sophie flushed with annoyance and pointedly devoted her attention to Lydia. Soon after that they arrived at the hotel.

The photographer had a tough time with the bridal couple. Although the hotel gardens were superb and the sun was shining, his clients refused to act like blissful newly marrieds. Sophie only came alive when the baby was in the picture and became as flexible as a stick of rock when Antonio had finally been induced to curve an arm round her. The photographer was not quite quick enough to hide his surprise at the complete absence of a bridal bouquet. Sophie said nothing, but the speaking glance that she cast in the groom's direction would have withered a less powerful personality.

Unaccustomed to such a ferocious lack of appreciation, Antonio looked so scornful when asked to smile tenderly down at Sophie that Sophie gritted her teeth and hissed like a spitting cat, 'Don't bother yourself!'

Silence simmered all the way to the airport. Sophie was more out of sorts than she could remember being in years, but not at all sure why she felt quite so angry and humiliated and wretched. Antonio received a melodramatic call from his current mistress. She asked him to deny the ridiculous rumour flying round that he, a Spanish noble of ancient lineage, had just got married to the British equivalent of trailer trash. What his mistress said in response to his icy rebuke in defence of his bride's honour led to her being unceremoniously dumped. At that point, Antonio truly felt himself to be a saint among men beset on all sides by unreasonable women.

At the airport, Sophie parted from Antonio to take care of Lydia's needs. She was engaged in changing Lydia into a fresh outfit when the public address system announced her name and asked her to go to a certain desk. Instant panic assailed Sophie. As she frantically finished dressing her niece she was convinced that something utterly ghastly had happened to Antonio. He had fallen down dead in the concourse and she had never got to say goodbye. Businessmen died of heart attacks all the time, didn't they? Antonio seemed to have so much money that he was a sure fire candidate for overwork and stress. On the other hand, perhaps she had been called to the desk to receive a message from Antonio. Could he have abandoned them at the airport because he just could not face taking the two of them back to Spain with him?

A helpless prey to her own fear, Sophie raced up with the buggy and identified herself with breathless urgency. But even as she did so she was frowning in surprise at the stockily built young man standing several feet away.

'Matt…?' she exclaimed. 'What are you doing here?'

Matt Moore went very red in the face. Inarticulate at the best of times, he pulled out the flowers he had been hiding behind his back and held the small bunch of candy-pink marguerites out to her like an offering.

'Oh, Matt…' Sophie said chokily, astonished that he had asked for her name to be announced.

'You come back and visit now,' Matt told her doggedly as she accepted the bouquet.

'Did you come all the way here just to tell me that?' Sophie gasped, tears burning her eyes and overflowing, for she was touched to the heart that he should have made so much effort when there was no prospect of reward. She reached for his hand and squeezed it tight, a sob catching in her throat.

'Look after yourself and Lydia,' Matt urged and then, without giving any hint of his intention, he gathered her into a clumsy bear-hug and kissed her.

It was as thrilling for Sophie as a wash with a wet flannel. But she felt very sorry for him and very guilty that in spite of all his nice qualities she had never fancied him. So she stood still and tolerated that one brief close-mouthed kiss because she could not bear to reject him yet again and it felt just then like the only consolation she could offer him.

Twenty feet away, Antonio was paralysed to the spot. He had headed to the relevant desk to investigate the instant he had heard Sophie's name being called. He had however believed that that message might have been intended for another Sophie with the same name. Now seeing her share a passionate embrace with Norah Moore's son, he felt betrayed beyond belief. She was his bride, his wife, the Marquesa de Salazar, and she was kissing another man and sobbing over him in a public place. His lean brown hands were clenched into furious fists of restraint. The dark, dangerous tide of rage consuming Antonio almost splintered through his hard self-control and provoked him into a violent intervention.

'Thanks for the flowers...see you some time.' Sophie pulled back from Matt and stoically resisted the temptation to wipe her mouth.

Barely a minute later, Antonio strode up while she was struggling to tighten Lydia's safety harness. She felt hot and bothered and messy and had been planning to steal five minutes to freshen up before rejoining him.

'Where did you come from?' Sophie enquired, pausing in her endeavours to throw a dirty look at the gorgeous blonde eyeing him up from across the concourse. It was far from being the first such appraisal Antonio had attracted. He turned heads, female heads in particular and far too many of them, Sophie acknowledged miserably. His spectacular dark good looks seemed to entitle him to the same attention a movie star might have expected. In her vulnerability, she was not alone. She wanted to lock him up in a cupboard or, at the very least, put a paper bag over his head.

'I heard your name over the public address system,' Antonio imparted, his attention welded to the lush fullness of her lower lip. He was very much taken aback by the fierce sting of desire that assailed him in spite of what he had witnessed.

'Oh...er, it was a friend just wanting to say goodbye,' Sophie mumbled, wrenching at the harness in frustration. 'I think this wretched thing is broken—'

'Allow me...' Antonio murmured flatly.

'It's very fiddly,' she warned him.

Antonio sorted it using only one hand. Somehow the sight of his easy success infuriated Sophie even more. In the VIP lounge, she sat feeding Lydia out of the jar of prepared food she had brought with her for emergency use.

'Couldn't that wait until we've boarded the jet?'

Antonio asked as though it were the height of bad taste to be seen feeding a baby.

Sophie shook her head and buttoned her soft pink mouth. She had to. If she hadn't she would have thrown a screaming fit. She had started the day with a crazy sense of adventure and happiness and her mood had gone steadily downhill ever since. Just then she was hitting rock-bottom. Antonio was gorgeous but she hated him. She hated fancying him like mad and she hated being married to him. At that moment she was convinced that a divorce from Antonio could not come quickly enough to satisfy her. She could have signed on the dotted line right there and then without a shred of regret.

He hadn't even bothered to offer her lunch at the hotel and her stomach was meeting her backbone. He had treated her like wallpaper most of the day. And when he wasn't treating her like wallpaper and ignoring her, he was either accusing her of doing something dreadful or criticising her. Sophie breathed in very deep, pent-up tears of self-pity clogging her throat. Here she was travelling off into the unknown to live in a different country, which was a quite terrifying prospect, and the only guy she had to depend on was behaving like an arrogant, insensitive bastard!

They boarded the private jet. Sophie cast a jaundiced eye over the luxury appointments and wondered what Antonio would do if she fainted from hunger. How bad would it make him feel? She reckoned she would have to die to get a real reaction from him. The jet took off. Her heart-shaped face adorned by two high spots of colour, Sophie was shown by the flight attendant into a sleeping compartment where a cot had already been secured in readiness for Lydia's occupation. She tucked her niece in for a nap and surveyed the opulent bed for the grown-ups. How many women had Antonio had in there? She bit her lip painfully and screwed her eyes up tight in a desperate attempt to hold back the tears ready to flood out. The level of her own distress shocked her.

Although it was rare for Antonio to touch alcohol before evening, he was contemplating the non-existent joys of matrimony over a brandy. Getting married had proved to be the hell he had always dimly suspected it would be. Sophie had allowed him to put a wedding ring on her finger and had then allowed another man to put his hands on her. That betrayal struck at the very roots of his masculinity and plunged Antonio right back into the same elemental rage that challenged his rapier-sharp thinking processes. His rational mind endeavoured to point out that it had been a kiss exchanged in public, but the conviction that passion had overpowered common sense and decency was not a consolation.

He pictured her tear-stained face afresh, her green eyes like wet jewels as she clutched that pathetic bunch of flowers. A heartbeat later she had had her arms wrapped round the vertically challenged gorilla from the run-down shop on the caravan site. As he recalled from his first visit when he had been looking for Sophie, the guy tended to grunt rather than speak, Antonio reflected with raging incredulity. He tipped his brandy back in one fiery gulp. Why had she not told him that she had a boyfriend? Did she think she loved the gorilla? Were grunts really that appealing? Why had she kept quiet about the relationship? Was she in fact expecting to continue the affair in secret? He set the glass down with a hard snap that sent a crack travelling up the crystal stem.

To his knowledge no Rocha wife had ever been unfaithful, although there had been a few rather unexpected deaths over the centuries. Death before dishonour. For the very first time Antonio found himself in sympathy with distant ancestors who had ridden off to war for months on end leaving young and beautiful wives behind at home. How was he supposed to go away for weeks on business? In the space of a moment, a new horrific dimension had been added to Antonio's outlook on matrimony. He tried to regard the potential problem of his bride's future behaviour as a basic security issue. Careful supervision and geographical location would reduce the chances of any similar offence occurring.

When Sophie returned to the main cabin, Antonio slid upright with the grace of a panther ready to spring at an unwary prey. Having looked her fill at his bold bronzed profile before he registered her reappearance, Sophie ostentatiously ignored him, screened a fake yawn and picked up a magazine for good measure.

'I saw you with Norah Moore's son at the airport,' Antonio murmured with icy cool.

'Did you?' Sophie was surprised but not concerned. 'Matt can be so kind and thoughtful. Maybe you assumed that I bought those flowers for myself. I *didn't*,' she declared with emphasis. 'Matt gave them to me.'

Antonio listened to that irrelevant and aggravating response with an amount of disbelief that did nothing to cool his ire. 'Do you seriously think that I am interested in where the flowers came from?' he enquired grittily.

'Oh, no, I'm sure you wouldn't be interested,' Sophie countered with a hint of acidity, still without having deigned to glance in his direction.

'Put the magazine down and look at me when you speak to me,' Antonio instructed grimly.

Sophie kept her attention on the magazine and turned a page very slowly and carefully. Antonio brought out a defiant streak in Sophie that had remained dormant and unknown even to her until she had met him. She wondered why it was that he had only to address her in a certain tone or raise an aristocratic eyebrow to excite her even temper to screaming pitch.

Provoked beyond bearing, Antonio swept up the magazine and slung it aside.

'So now you're going to add bullying to all your other sins,' Sophie commented in a tone of immense martyrdom. 'I can't say I'm surprised—'

'What other sins?' Antonio raked at her incredulously.

'Oh, let's not get into that right now,' Sophie advised, rising to her full, unimposing height and pausing to hurriedly cram her feet back into the high heels she had removed. 'Unless you've got all day to listen. And, of course, even if you did magically have the time or the good manners to listen, I might drop dead from hunger first.'

'Hunger?' Antonio growled, black brows pleating.

'Obviously I shall have to get used to my comfort being ignored in favour of yours. I haven't eaten since eight this morning and I am starving,' Sophie tossed back at him accusingly. 'And you couldn't care less, could you? Because you've made it very clear that if you're not hungry, I'm not supposed to be hungry either!'

'The detour back to the hotel for the photographic session meant that there wasn't time for lunch,' Antonio informed her drily, striving not to notice how the vivid colour of anger enhanced the brightness of her eyes.

Sophie folded her arms and sent a flashing look of scorn at him. 'So, in other words, starving me was deliberate—'

'How the hell do you make that out?' Antonio launched back at her wrathfully.

'I argued about the photographs being cancelled and that annoyed you and so lunch went off the menu—'

'How could you think that I am capable of being that petty?' Antonio's disgust at the allegation was convincing. 'I did not wish to reschedule our flight. For that reason I arranged for a meal to be served to us now.'

Chagrin rather than relief at that news gripped Sophie. 'Couldn't you have explained that to me back at the hotel?'

'You were sulking—'

'I don't sulk!' Sophie hurled.

'—and if you want to sulk like a little girl you will be treated like one,' Antonio completed without hesitation, while wondering how she would react if he just lifted her off her absurdly high-heeled shoes and kissed her into merciful silence.

'Try that on me again and you'll see what happens!' Sophie threw feverishly.

Infuriated by the weird thoughts and ideas interfering with his concentration, Antonio resisted the temptation to rise to her bait. Stunning dark eyes cool as a winter lake, he surveyed her with intimidating self-command. 'I believe you think that you can distract me from your own inexcusable behaviour at the airport. You haven't a prayer on that score. I saw you kissing Norah Moore's son.'

Sophie went pink and jerked a thin shoulder and studied the floor for about twenty seconds. That sufficed for the amount of discomfiture she experienced at that assurance. Indeed after the heartbreakingly hurtful day she had endured she was actually quite pleased that he had been forced to register that one man at least had thought her worthy of his attention. She glanced up again, green eyes rebellious. 'So?' she queried.

Antonio was incredulous at that unapologetic reaction. 'Do not dare to treat it as nothing,' he warned her, his accent thick with anger. 'Sharing a very public embrace with your lover on the day you became my wife is not acceptable behaviour by any standards.'

Her defiance ebbed a little and she squirmed, no longer able to meet his proud dark golden eyes. 'For goodness' sake, Matt's not my lover or *my* anything—'

'I know what I saw,' Antonio incised icily.

'Matt's fancied me for ages but I only ever thought of him as a friend,' Sophie admitted reluctantly, angry at being forced to make an explanation. 'He was upset about me marrying you and he came to the airport to say goodbye. I couldn't face rejecting him again. I like him and I felt sorry for him, so I put up with him kissing me!'

'I might have found that a convincing story if you hadn't been weeping all over him when I saw you,' Antonio derided with a curled lip.

In that instant, temper and hurt reached flashpoint inside Sophie. 'I was crying because you had made me so miserable!'

'I had made you miserable?' Antonio repeated in thunderous disbelief. 'What had I done?'

'Matt being upset about me leaving and giving me those flowers was the first nice thing that happened to me today. Think about that, Antonio...this was supposed to be my wedding day. And it's been totally horrible!' Sophie condemned tearfully, all the wounded feelings she had suppressed throughout the day suddenly coalescing and finally making sense to her.

'How has it been horrible?' Antonio demanded fiercely.

'I'll probably never have another wedding day,' Sophie proclaimed grittily, pride helping her to swallow back the tears that had been threatening. 'I know it couldn't have been romantic in the circumstances, but you could at least have made it pleasant and friendly. I spent two whole days trailing round London finding this outfit and you couldn't even tell me that I looked OK—'

Dark blood had risen to emphasise the sculpted line of his hard cheekbones. 'I—'

'It's OK…don't worry about it. Do you think I haven't worked out for myself that I couldn't ever reach your standards? But I made the effort; I *tried.* You didn't even try to be nice. You accused me of tipping off the reporters at the church. You didn't give me flowers or anything and the entire time you acted like being with me and Lydia was just one big, awful bore. Matt was so sweet and the comparison between you and him was too much—'

'The comparison between me and that gorilla?' Antonio grated between clenched teeth, seizing on that line because her previous comments had hit too many raw nerves in succession to even be considered in the midst of an argument.

'You're a hateful snob,' Sophie told him fiercely. 'You treat me like dirt…but he treats me like I'm something special!'

A brisk knock sounded on the door and broke the silence that fell in the wake of that last bitter rebuke. A flight attendant entered with a trolley of food. Sophie dropped her head, heavy curls tumbling across her delicate profile to conceal her tear-wet eyes from notice. Trembling with emotion, she sank back down into her seat and cringed over the last revealing words she had flung at him. *You treat me like dirt…he treats me like I'm something special!*

Why don't you be honest with yourself? a snide little voice was mocking inside her head. The truth, which she only recognised in retrospect, cut her pride to ribbons. Her wedding day had been a disaster because she had forgotten it was a 'deal' rather than a joyous occasion to be celebrated. She had got carried away with bridal fervour. She had absolutely craved personal attention and notice from Antonio. She would have crawled over broken glass for a single compliment. Her distress had stemmed from her pain and disappointment when he had neglected to meet her unrealistic hopes and treated her like wallpaper instead.

Did she have the right to complain about the way he had treated her? Or was she being unfair to him? After all, it hadn't been a real wedding for two people who cared about each other. Antonio didn't care two straws about her and she had to learn to live with that, didn't she? Someone like him was never, ever going to think of someone like her as special, she thought wretchedly. Having to put up with her all day had probably been a taxing enough challenge for him. Her aching throat convulsed. She stared down at the inviting meal that had been laid before her and discovered that she was no longer hungry. A tear rolled down her cheek and splashed onto the plate.

'Sophie…' Antonio breathed tautly.

'Leave me alone!' she gasped strickenly and, scrambling up, she fled down the aisle and vanished into the sleeping compartment.

CHAPTER SIX

BY THE time that Antonio entered the compartment Sophie was fast asleep. Curled up in a ball, tawny-blonde curls tumbling over a delicate cheekbone, she looked very young, incredibly pretty and alarmingly vulnerable.

She was also his wife. *His wife.* It was a disturbing moment of truth for Antonio. She was now Sophie Cunningham de Rocha, the Marquesa de Salazar. She had had grounds for complaint, he acknowledged, his handsome mouth hardening on that admission of self-blame. He was not accustomed to finding himself in the wrong. But he had censured her behaviour as his wife without once accepting her right to be treated as though she was his wife.

A slight movement in the cot attracted his attention. He glanced down and met Lydia's big hopeful brown eyes. The baby flashed him a huge gummy smile of welcome and wriggled with excess energy. Without words, Lydia was letting him know that she wanted out of the cot and that she was expecting him to supply the means of her escape from captivity. He was amused until the baby let out a little bleating cry of disappointment when he turned back to the door.

'If I took you out of there, I wouldn't know what to do with you,' Antonio pointed out in his own defence.

The melting brown eyes stayed pinned to him.

'Yes, of course I can learn, but in easy stages,' Antonio murmured in what he was hoped was a soothing tone that might send her back to sleep. He took another step away from the cot.

The brown eyes glistened and the rosebud mouth trembled piteously.

At the threat of tears, Antonio tensed. He glanced back at Sophie, who was clearly enjoying the very sound sleep of exhaustion. Breathing in deep and mustering his legendary ability to deal with the unexpected, he reached down to lift Lydia out of the cot. She wriggled with pleasure and smiled like mad at him in return.

'You know how to get your own way,' Antonio informed the baby wryly. 'But success is not always followed by the reward you expect. We're going to watch the business news together.'

Sophie wakened only when her shoulder was gently shaken. Feathery lashes lifting, she focused slowly on Antonio's darkly handsome face and her mouth ran dry. Try as she might, she could not suppress her response to his mesmeric attraction.

'You may want to get up,' he murmured softly. 'We'll be landing in fifteen minutes. Did you sleep well?'

'I don't remember even putting my head down,' she confided, glancing down at her watch. 'I'm amazed Lydia let me sleep this long!'

'I've been entertaining her.'

Before she could comment on that surprising information, he had gone. Ten minutes later she joined him in the main cabin. Lydia was enjoying a peaceful nap in her baby harness, a sure-fire sign of contentment.

'How did you manage with her?' Sophie asked uncomfortably.

'Consuela, one of the crew, is a parent. She lent me some assistance when Lydia needed a drink,' Antonio admitted modestly. 'But Lydia was very good and easily amused.'

'Thanks for letting me sleep.' Sophie studied her linked hands and cleared her throat. 'I owe you an apology for the way I lost my temper earlier.'

'No, you don't owe me anything,' Antonio contradicted with quiet assurance. 'You were right to complain and I am sorry that I made the day a difficult one. I must confess that I was nourishing a certain resentment of the situation which I needed to deal with.'

It came entirely naturally to Sophie to reach across the aisle to touch his lean brown hand with her own in an instinctive gesture of sympathetic understanding. 'Of course you felt bitter, but you don't have to apologise for being human. It must've been so hard for someone like you to put up with a brother like Pablo. Then to be landed with responsibility for Lydia into the bargain, well, obviously you felt fed up.'

That sudden gush of generosity from her corner was too much for Antonio's innate reserve about his own feelings. His expression of regret, honest admission of fault and the explanation he had believed she was due had cost him dearly. Her unexpected compassion stung his strong pride like acid.

'You mistook my meaning,' Antonio replied icily. 'Never at any time since I learned of my niece's existence have I wished that her care fell to someone else. There is no more proper person than I to undertake that task and I would never attempt to avoid the responsibility. I don't expect you to understand it, but loyalty to my family is as integral a part of me as my honour.'

Sophie coloured hot pink and then white, mortification at that unabashed snub biting at her frail self-esteem. No matter how hard she tried she always seemed to say or do the wrong thing with Antonio, she reflected wretchedly. He appeared to believe that she was too vulgar and common to comprehend the more refined sensibilities of a Spanish aristocrat.

'That's a hateful thing to say,' she whispered with scorching fervour, for once again he had hurt her. 'I was every bit as loyal to Belinda as you are to your precious family!'

An hour later, she was seated in a long, opulent limousine being driven through the Andalusian countryside. Up until that point she had rigorously ignored or crushed Antonio's conversational attempts to redeem himself.

When he tried to tell her a little about the history of Spain, Sophie said tartly, 'Save yourself the trouble. Buy me the book!'

When the country road wended through silvery olive groves, Antonio informed her that they were now on the family estate. After what felt like a very long time to Sophie, the olive trees gave way to orange orchards and a picturesque whitewashed village straggling over the lower slopes of forested hills. Locals peered out of the houses and stopped in the narrow, winding street to stare at the limousine and wave acknowledgement.

'Are we still on your family estate?' Rampant curiosity finally forced Sophie to abandon her stony silence and ask that question as the limo traversed a shaded road surrounded on all sides by dense evergreen woods.

'*Sí.* My great-great-grandfather planted those oak trees,' Antonio told her with unhidden pride.

'It's like the fairy tale of Puss-in-Boots,' Sophie muttered helplessly and, when Antonio angled a look of incomprehension at her, added, 'Puss-in-Boots wanted to impress the king with the idea that his master was hugely important and rich. So, he pretended all the land they passed belonged to this character he made up called the Marquis of Carabas.'

'The Marquis of Carabas,' Antonio repeated with only the slightest tremor of amusement disturbing his dark deep drawl.

'Of course that marquis belongs in the fairy story and he was only for pretend and you're real,' Sophie conceded absently. 'But all this feels very unreal to me…'

There was a reason for the way she suddenly fell silent. The limousine had turned a corner and through the trees she caught a glimpse of an ancient stone building. Adorned with as many towers and turrets as any palace in a fairy tale, it sat in an oasis of lush green vegetation. It was indescribably beautiful and she was enchanted from that first moment.

'What do you think?'

Sophie veiled her stunned eyes and shrugged with studied casualness, too self-conscious to display her true reactions. 'It's very big…I'm not going to be tripping over you every five minutes, am I?'

'It's unlikely. Perhaps I should have mentioned before now that a nanny has been engaged to help you care for Lydia,' Antonio advanced with caution.

'As long as I like the nanny, that's fine with me.' Sophie was grateful that an extra pair of hands would be available. All too often she had been forced to rely on Norah Moore's good nature. A nanny to help out with Lydia would be a real luxury.

The limo came to a halt in a timeless courtyard ornamented with palm trees in vast pots. The soft sunlight of evening illuminated the stone arches and columns that made an arcade on three sides. Water droplets sparkled and fell from the fountain that played near the massive wooden doors that stood ajar on a floor that, even at a distance of several feet, was clearly polished to a mirror finish.

Lydia supported on one slight hip, Sophie crossed the threshold and froze at the sight of the throng of people filling the giant entrance hall.

With wonderful assurance, Antonio cupped a light hand below her elbow and drew her on to greet an elegant little old lady who might have been chipped out of frozen granite.

'My grandmother, Doña Ernesta…Sophie.'

Doña Ernesta gave a regal nod and said that it was a great joy to welcome her grandson, his bride and her great-granddaughter home. Sophie was not deceived. She knew that she was about as welcome in her role as Antonio's bride as the bad fairy. Attention was quickly focused on Lydia, who was greeted with a sincere warmth that quite transformed her great-grandmother's frozen granite exterior. A young smiling nanny was brought forward, introduced, and Lydia was handed over to an enthusiastic reception.

'Come and meet the rest of the staff,' Antonio urged Sophie then, ignoring her dismay as she registered just how many people appeared to fall within that category.

Everyone who worked inside the *castillo* was waiting to pay their respects. Antonio carried her through the introductions with the sure confidence that seemed to accompany everything he did and she really appreciated his support.

Afterwards he closed his hand over hers and walked her up the carved stone staircase. 'You must be incredibly hungry,' he murmured.

'Yes…I should've eaten when I got the chance.' Sophie sighed, her attention locking to the ancient stone walls and gothic arches surrounding them. It was a real castle, a one hundred per cent genuine medieval castle, and she was fascinated by it.

His handsome mouth quirked at her fatalistic outlook. 'I upset you. In the hope that you'll forgive that I've arranged for a meal to be served in your suite. I want you to be happy here at the *castillo*.'

'Your grandmother wouldn't agree with you.'

'It's a shame that she didn't have the opportunity to get to know you at your sister's wedding, *querida*. She would never be unkind and will soon become accustomed to our marriage.'

Sophie was less confident.

'By the way, I should warn you that I have told no one of our marital agreement. Secrets shared soon lead to a wider circle becoming acquainted with what was once private—'

'You mean Doña Ernesta thinks we're like…*really* married?' Sophie interrupted in dismay. 'You should tell her the truth!'

'It would only complicate matters. Allow me to know my own family best. To all intents and purposes it is wisest if at this point at least our marriage appears to be normal,' Antonio decreed.

Sophie disagreed but took the hint. It was obvious to her that Doña Ernesta was hopping with rage and disappointment over the fact that her grandson appeared to have thrown his title, his wealth and his giant castle away on a penniless nobody from England. Sophie did not blame his grandmother one little bit for her annoyance. Antonio was just about the equivalent of a prince and a prince deserved a princess.

Upstairs, Antonio showed her into a beautifully furnished and enormous sitting room, which led into a huge bedroom that in turn had a fabulous bathroom and dressing room attached.

'All this is just for me?' she gasped.

'Dinner will be served here in forty minutes,' he imparted.

'Here...? ' Her relief was palpable. She had been afraid that she might have to dress up to eat in some fancy dining room and she had nothing suitable to change into.

'*Sí.* I've organised an informal meal of your favourite foods—'

'But you don't know what I like...'

'I phoned Mrs Moore to find out, *querida*.' Antonio gazed down at her, stunning dark golden eyes very serious. 'You have eaten hardly anything today. That's my fault. I want you to relax and feel comfortable at the *castillo*.'

Sophie vented an awkward laugh. 'I'm never going to relax in a place like this!'

'Of course you will,' Antonio declared, long brown fingers tilting up her chin to persuade her to look up again. 'You're my wife and this is your home and you must treat it as such. Your comfort is of prime importance to me and to our staff.'

For a long, timeless moment, she was conscious only of the spectacular power of his gaze. His concern for her sent a sudden dangerous flare of happiness winging through her slight frame. The faint citrusy aroma of the shaving lotion he used flared her nostrils. She wanted to drink the scent in like a drug, for it was already wonderfully familiar to her. Something tightened low in her pelvis and an awareness so acute it hurt seemed to make every inch of her feel unbearably sensitive. She wanted to lean closer to him, retain that fleeting physical contact of his fingers against her throat. But she rebelled against her weakness and literally forced herself back for him with a brittle smile fixed to her flushed face. 'Right, so if I'm to make myself at home, I'll have a bath before the food arrives,' she framed not quite steadily. 'So first you'd better tell me where Lydia is, because I want to check she's OK without me.'

For a split second, Antonio was very taut as he mastered the raw hunger that had leapt as high as a burning brand in him. All it had taken was her proximity and that reference to a bath and his imagination had gone crazy. His gleaming gaze veiled while he fought an outrageous desire to simply grab her like a Neanderthal cave dweller. Lust had never controlled him to such an extent that he almost forgot who he was. Exhilarated by the very power of that sensation, he suspended all rational thought on the issue.

It was sex, just sex, nothing to get worked up about. She was amazingly sexy and the very fact that she didn't even seem to appreciate the strength of her own attraction only added to her appeal. He could not recall when he had last been with a woman capable of walking past a mirror without looking in it. Not to mention one so devoted to a baby's interests that her own needs took second billing.

Sophie peeped in on Lydia, who was blissfully asleep in a large cot. Her niece was being watched over by what appeared to be a good half of the female staff. A little while later, her concern laid to rest, Sophie sank into the warm, scented water of the sunken bath that had so captured her interest. She rested her head back against the built-in pillow and surveyed the other luxurious fittings with impressed-to-death eyes. She could see that the misery of being married to Antonio was going to be alleviated by certain small consolations. So, she couldn't have him and other women were going to have him…*but*, she rushed to remind herself, she had Lydia, a bath to die for and at least the promise of food. On the downside this was her wedding night and she was alone? So what was new about being alone, she asked herself, struggling not to give way to self-pity. Unhappily she was all too well aware that Antonio would never have left a princess alone…

Thoroughly refreshed, Sophie emerged from the bathroom with a white towel knotted round her and a riot of tousled curls falling round her shoulders. Her nose twitched at the faint enticing aroma in the air and she followed it.

Antonio was standing by the balcony doors in the sitting room.

'Oh!' Sophie jerked to a disconcerted halt a few feet from the table that was now set with sparkling glasses and cutlery and the catering trolley standing by. 'Did *you* bring the food?'

Antonio was immediately aware that he was staring. With her blonde hair in damp disarray, her fair skin pink and only a towel screening her slim curves between breast and knee, she looked incredibly appealing. 'No…I'm here to dine with you.'

Sophie stared back at him in surprise.

'If we're hoping to pretend that this is a normal relationship, we can't spend our wedding night in different rooms,' Antonio pointed out.

'Oh, right…yeah,' Sophie mumbled, appreciating that he was only joining her because he had no choice in the matter. That meant that his presence was nothing to get thrilled about. 'I'd better get dressed, then.'

Antonio resisted a schoolboyish urge to tell her that

he thought she looked great just as she was and countered with studied casualness, 'A robe will do.'

'I don't have one and it's too warm for my jeans. I don't have much else yet—'

'Just stay as you are,' Antonio suggested huskily.

The simmering tension in the air danced along her nerve endings. He had changed as well, into black chinos, which accentuated his long, powerful legs, and a casual but very elegant blue open-necked shirt. He managed to look impossibly sophisticated and gorgeous.

'You don't look as stuffy as you usually do!' Sophie exclaimed before she could think better of such frankness.

Faint colour demarcated the spectacular cheekbones that gave his lean bronzed face such intense power and beauty of line. Stuffy? His keen intellect threw up every possible meaning and none was complimentary. It was a word he associated with some of his more stodgy relatives, the ones boringly trapped in convention and habit. Was that how he seemed to her? *Stuffy?* She was seven years younger than he was. Was it such a gap?

'We should eat,' Antonio murmured flatly, determined not to react to what he knew had been a thoughtless remark.

Sophie knew she had offended. 'It's just the way you talk and the suits… I'm not used to businessmen and I guess all of them wear suits—'

'What way do I talk?' Antonio discovered that he could not silence that question as he spun out a chair for her to sit down.

'I really didn't mean to suggest anything critical,' Sophie muttered anxiously, sitting down on the very edge of the upholstered antique dining chair. 'You've got fantastic manners and of course you can't help being formal… I mean you're a marquis—'

'And stuffy,' Antonio breathed and shrugged, the ultimate gesture of Mediterranean cool, but that word she had used had been etched like acid into his soul. 'Let's eat.'

Sophie leapt up to examine the contents of the trolley and exclaimed in delight at the sight of the barbecued ribs, pizza and French fries. A multitude of other options was also available. 'You have an in-house takeaway?'

'I wanted you to have food you felt comfortable with.'

'I eat loads of more healthy things too, but Norah wouldn't have had a clue about that. To be honest, Norah and Matt eat stuff like this most of the time. I only like it occasionally.' As she spoke Sophie was scooping up cushions and throws and piling them on the carpet in an untidy heap. Then she flung open the balcony doors on the cooling night air.

In a trice the superbly elegant room became disorganised and yet more full of life. It dawned on Antonio that sitting at a table when the hard wooden floor was available might be deemed stuffy. While Sophie emptied the trolley and knelt down among the cushions to arrange containers and plates in the style of an impromptu indoor picnic, he uncorked the champagne and filled the flutes. She ate without cutlery, licking her fingertips clean like a delicate cat. She tore a strip off the pizza, tipped her head back and bit off tiny pieces. Never until that moment had it occurred to him that watching a woman eat could be a sensual experience. He was absolutely fascinated.

'What would you like to talk about?' she asked cheerfully, flopping back against the piled-up pillows to finish her champagne.

'My stuffy good manners prevented me from asking how you and your sister came to have different fathers,' Antonio admitted.

Sophie tensed, but tried to laugh off her discomfiture. 'Oh, that's no big deal. Belinda's father was married to our mother, Isabel. He was an oil executive and he wasn't home much. Isabel met my father when he was painting their house—'

'He was an artist?'

'He painted walls, not pictures,' Sophie told him thinly. 'Well, he got her pregnant with me and she left her husband for him…'

'And?' Antonio prompted as the silence dragged.

'My father was no great catch and Isabel soon realised her mistake. When I was a month old, she went back to her husband and left me behind with Dad.'

'That must have been hard for your father—'

'Dad would do just about anything for money and Isabel sent him money every month until I was sixteen. She never visited me. Apart from the handouts, she just blanked out the whole affair like it and I never happened.' Sophie tipped up her chin, a defiant glint in her expressive green eyes.

'She was probably ashamed of what she had done,' Antonio murmured gently, seeing the pain that she was struggling to hide. Reaching over, he linked his fingers with hers in a comforting gesture that was as instinctive as it was unusual for him. 'You did very well without her, *querida*.'

'You really think so?' Antonio was so close that Sophie could hardly catch her breath.

'You bend but you don't break,' Antonio breathed a

little thickly, leaning over her to let a soothing fingertip score the soft pink fullness of her lower lip in a touch as light as silk.

The faintest suspicion of a breeze was ruffling the curls against her shoulder. She was very still, heart pumping like crazy below the towel. Her breasts felt tight and confined and a restive energy was filtering through her. Her whole focus was on him. If he didn't kiss her she thought she might die from the cruel disappointment of it.

A masculine thumb brushed against a springy blonde loop of hair in a movement so subtle she wasn't quite sure it had happened. His scorching golden eyes collided with hers and the knot of tension deep down inside her tightened. 'I love your hair…it has a life of its own.'

'Antonio…' she whispered, stretching back against the pillows, letting her head fall back, bright corkscrew curls spilling out and catching the light of the sinking sun. She felt shameless but she was being driven by a craving much stronger than she was.

His breath fanned her cheek. He took his time and let his mouth toy with hers. Longing snaked through her in a fierce, almost frightening surge. Without even knowing what she was about to do she pulled him down to her. He resisted and laughed huskily, gazed down at her with shimmering dark golden eyes full of satisfaction.

'I don't respond well to the whip and chair approach,' he mocked.

She felt foolish and exposed and temper leapt into the chasm. In a split second she had rolled away and sat up. 'I'm not a joke!'

Stunned by the immediacy of her rejection, Antonio sprang up in concert. '*Por dios*, I was teasing—'

'No, you weren't...you were crowing!' Sophie accused tempestuously. 'Well, before you get carried away with the idea that I'm too enthusiastic—'

Antonio reached out and tugged her straight back into his arms. 'You firebrand...you could never be *too* enthusiastic for me. You turn me on so hard and so fast that I can't think this close to you,' he admitted in a roughened undertone.

On the brink of fighting loose again, Sophie paused and fixed huge anxious green eyes on his lean, strong face. 'Truthfully?'

He spread long brown fingers to frame her cheekbones and his hands were not quite steady. 'I'm burning for you, *querida*.'

She felt the truth of it in his raw urgency and she trembled. 'Then stop playing games—'

'I'm not playing.' Antonio claimed a long, hard, potent kiss that made her grip his arms for support and left her head swimming. 'Believe me, I didn't bargain on this—'

'You can't plan everything—'

'But I *do*,' he growled in frustration, coming back for another fierce and hungry taste of her. 'This shouldn't be happening—'

Her small fingers delved into his luxuriant black hair to pull his head back. 'Then...stop!'

His smouldering golden gaze struck sparks from hers. 'I can't...I wanted you the first time I saw you nearly three years ago. Now I want you even more.'

At that admission, her troubled eyes shone like stars and she screened them. But she still wanted to shout her joy from the rooftops. What he felt wasn't love, but then she had never hoped for love from Antonio. His desire was enough to satisfy her deep, desperate need for some kind of response from him. It wouldn't last, naturally it wouldn't, she thought feverishly. But a desire to match her own was there for the taking now and she was not too proud to seize the moment.

He crushed her lush lips beneath his again. The sweet, stabbing invasion of his tongue in the tender reaches of her mouth made her gasp out loud. He lifted her effortlessly up in his arms and carried her into the bedroom. His strength left her breathless. Resting her down on the bed, he undid the towel. Unprepared for that instant unveiling, she crossed her arms over her nakedness in an instinctive movement.

Antonio surveyed her startled eyes and hot cheeks in surprise. 'You can't be shy with me…'

'I'm not shy,' Sophie denied to the best of her ability, taking advantage of his momentary stasis to shimmy away. Pulling back the bedding, she slid speedily under it with more than a suggestion of a crab scuttling below a rock for cover. 'Not the slightest bit shy,' she added with determined emphasis, and she sat up to embark on the buttons on his shirt in an effort to distract him.

'Let me look at you, then.' Antonio closed long fingers into the sheet she had wrapped below her arms and tugged it down before she could even guess his intent. The tantalising jut of her pert breasts provoked a ragged groan of appreciation from him. He caught her to him with one powerful arm, bent her back against him and explored the firm creamy swells with unashamed expertise. His slightest touch set her tender flesh on fire. Her teeth clenched, her hips shifting on the sheet beneath her. When he toyed with the rosy crests that were swollen and sensitised by his attention, she was unable to suppress the moan rising in her throat.

'You're even more beautiful than I thought you

would be, *querida*,' Antonio breathed thickly, hungry dark golden eyes welded with all-male admiration to the ripe, rounded curves he had revealed. 'And a hundred times more responsive.'

Straightening up to his full height, he finished unbuttoning his shirt and peeled it off. As he shifted position sleek, strong muscles flexed in his strong brown torso and accentuated the powerful breadth of his chest and the rock-hard flatness of his abdomen. Ebony curls liberally shaded his pectorals. She pulled in a sudden gulp of air to her starved lungs. Her heartbeat had quickened to a pulsing thump behind her breastbone: he was spectacularly male. She couldn't drag her mesmerised attention from him until he unzipped his trousers and embarrassment claimed her, forcing her to drop her gaze.

'Come here,' Antonio urged softly.

She scrambled up on her knees, glancing up at him from below her curling lashes, her face burning from the awareness of her nudity. With a husky groan, he just reached for her as though she were a doll. With his hands spread across the feminine swell of her hips, he raised her higher and clamped her hard up against his lean muscular frame. Warm and silky smooth and interestingly rough, his body was an electrifying mix of different textures against her softer skin. She was insanely aware of the hot, hard thrust of his erection and of her own feverish yearning for his touch. She felt programmed, enslaved by the wanton promise of the pleasure he had already given her.

'Touch me,' she mumbled shakily.

'Until you beg me to stop.' He tumbled her back across the bed and came down to her, strong and bronzed and pagan in his sexual intensity. He lowered his proud dark head to the prominent pink buds of her breasts and let his tongue lash the straining tips. She arched her spine and cried out when he intensified that sensation with the graze of his teeth and his knowing mouth. Heat burned low in her pelvis.

'Don't stop,' she whispered urgently, shifting her hips in a restive movement against the sheet, wildly, wickedly conscious of the growing ache at the very heart of her.

Golden eyes molten with desire, Antonio parted her thighs. With sure skill he parted the cluster of curls crowning her womanhood and touched her where she had never been touched before. That intimacy smashed her tenuous control to pieces. He found the most sensitive spot in her entire body and a burning, drowning sweetness of sensation took hold of her and blanked out all other awareness. As the twisting spiral of pleasure tightened to the edge of near pain inside her, she writhed.

'Antonio…' His name was like a prayer on her lips. She could no longer contain the wildness sweeping over her in potent waves. Her hips squirmed up in a sinuous rhythm as old as time, tiny whimpers breaking low in her throat.

'*Enamorada*…you intoxicate me,' he confessed fiercely as he came over her. 'I intend to give you more pleasure than anyone has ever given you.'

When he drove into the slick, wet depths of her, excitement roared through her every skin cell with the ferocity of a forest fire. The sudden sharp pain induced by that bold invasion took her entirely by surprise. Her eyes widened in shock and she muffled her involuntary cry against his shoulder.

Antonio stilled and looked down at her. 'Did I hurt you?'

'No...'

He stared down at the luminous clarity of her beautiful eyes. 'I know I hurt you,' he breathed huskily. 'Was I too rough?'

Hot pink washed her hairline, for she was mortified but far too proud and cautious to admit that he was her first lover. 'Of course not—'

'You excite me beyond all control,' Antonio confessed thickly, sinking by slow, skilled degrees into her now more receptive body. 'I forgot how small you are, how fragile.'

His every subtle movement engulfed her in hot, sweet pleasure. The tempo stepped up. Passion gripped her in a flashing surge of high-voltage sensation. He sank his hands below her hips and tipped her up to him, plunging back into her with raw, demanding urgency. Her heart hammered and she fought to breathe in short little spurts. Need and excitement had combined and the ache for fulfilment was a torment. Her hunger peaked in a shattering release. Losing herself in the voluptuous shock waves of convulsive pleasure, she cried out in joy and amazement.

In the aftermath, Antonio curved her round him, kissed the top of her head and studied the ornate ceiling with brilliant golden eyes. He had both arms wrapped round her in a possessive hold. He had never had such fantastic sex. And she was his, signed, sealed, delivered, even ringed. He wanted to punch the air and shout. Indeed he felt hugely satisfied with life in general. He had ditched a mistress who had been downright boring and, if truth be told, a whiner, only to discover that his bride had a magnificent gift for passion. And unless he was very much mistaken his bride had brought him a very special gift that he had never dreamt he might receive on his wedding night: she had been a virgin. He thought that was absolutely amazing. He thought it was fate that she had miraculously conserved her perfect body for him. He did indeed owe her a humble apology for assuming the worst that night he had seen her coming off the beach. At about that point he remembered their agreement and he was stunned that he could have forgotten it…

Sophie was happy. In fact she could never recall feeling quite so happy except of course in those dreams she sometimes recalled when she first wakened. Wonderful dreams in which she wandered hand in hand through sunlit places with Antonio. Antonio had had a starring role in her best dreams for so long that he was almost a fixture there. And now she had learned that he lived up to every secret fantasy she had ever had about what he might be like in bed. His future in her dreams was now assured for a lifetime, she conceded buoyantly and snuggled closer.

For the first time in almost three years she was letting herself recall the fact that she loved Antonio. Although he was destined never to know it, he had stolen her heart at their first meeting. She had yet to decide what she found most attractive about him. His cleverness, his looks, his wonderful manners, his fabulous smile? Whatever, even though she had known even then that loving him was stupid, no rival had managed to supplant him. That was why she was so oversensitive and prone to losing her temper around Antonio, she acknowledged ruefully. He could hurt her so easily and when it came to him she lost all common sense. Did that explain why she had just given her virginity to a male who had announced up front that he wanted to be a womaniser at the same time as he pretended to be a husband? So what was he pretending to be now? Her happy feelings dive-bombed faster than the speed of the light.

Antonio decided that he was doing far too much thinking. Why complicate things? Why look for trouble that wasn't there? He rolled Sophie off his chest, confined her beneath one powerful arm and kissed her breathless. 'You should have warned me that you were a virgin, *querida*,' he told her softly. 'I could have made it less painful.'

Emerging from a kiss that made her head swim and her toes curl, Sophie was aghast at that comment, for it meant that he had noticed what she had assumed he would not. 'What gives you the idea that I was a virgin?' She forced a laugh, for she was convinced that there was no way he could know for sure. 'I mean, how likely is that at my age?'

'Very unlikely,' Antonio agreed silkily, pinning her against the pillows and rearranging her into a rather more intimate position. 'But please don't get the idea that I'm complaining about your lack of form in the bedroom—'

'No?' Sophie's interruption was a little jerky because her teeth were gritted. That reference to 'form' which was normally applied to a horse and its racing performance, struck her as the ultimate in humiliation. Any minute now he'd be slapping her on the rump and offering her extra oats.

In fact Antonio seemed delighted that she had proved to be a complete novice in the sex stakes. But Sophie was unnerved and mortified by the speed with which he had deduced that reality. If she didn't watch out he would soon be questioning the significance of why she had yielded her precious virginity to him. He would guess that she was a lot keener on him than appearances might suggest. And if that happened, she knew she would die a thousand deaths from shame and never look him in the face again.

'Not at all, *enamorada*,' Antonio confirmed with lazy cool, running a confident and appreciative hand along the quivering line of one slender thigh. 'I suspect we're going to have a huge amount of fun filling in the blanks in your education.'

Employing all the self-control she could muster, Sophie pulled back from him. 'You've got me *so* wrong. I may have acted the innocent to amuse myself, but there is just no way I was a virgin and I can't believe you should think that I was.'

'Why are you trying to deny the obvious? Why should you be embarrassed about the fact that you didn't sleep around? Why would you want to persuade me otherwise?' Brilliant golden eyes full of incomprehension rested on her. 'I think that you being a virgin on our wedding night is an amazing achievement. You should be proud.'

Her small hands coiled into fierce fists. He knew what he knew and her secret was a secret no more. Her clumsy attempt to blow dust over her tracks had failed. His awareness that he had been her first lover made her feel horribly exposed and vulnerable. Gripped by the growing suspicion that she had behaved very stupidly with him, she scrambled out of the bed.

Snatching up the towel on the floor, she dragged it round herself again as though it were her only cover in a life-threatening storm. 'Look, stop going on about it!'

'Come back to bed,' Antonio murmured as gently as if he were dealing with a wild creature.

'No, been there, done that,' Sophie slung with jewel bright green eyes full of angry defiance, dull coins of pink burning over her cheekbones. 'You were great and you did me a favour, but let's leave it at that!'

'A favour?' At that contemptuous dismissal, Antonio went rigid and any desire to humour and soothe left him.

CHAPTER SEVEN

'YOU said I did you a favour. Explain what you mean by that,' Antonio instructed with lethal cool.

Playing for time, Sophie dragged in a ragged breath. 'Can't you guess?'

Hard dark golden eyes rested on her with uncompromising force. 'Answer my question, *por favor.*'

'OK.' Sophie lifted and dropped her slim shoulders, attempting to strike a casual note while she frantically plumbed her imagination for a suitable explanation. She was totally terrified that Antonio would guess why he had found it so easy to get her into bed. 'I set you up,' she claimed daringly.

Unimpressed, Antonio elevated an aristocratic black brow. '*No me diga*...you don't say!'

His apparent calm only made her more desperate than ever to save face. 'I'm nearly twenty-three years old and I thought it was way past time I stopped being a virgin,' she spelt out, 'so I picked you to do the deed.'

That brazen claim hit home and outrage powered through Antonio. 'You did...*what*?' he raked at her in raw disbelief.

The atmosphere could have been cut with a knife and Sophie was so nervous she was trembling. Forced to defend her story, she paled. 'You've been around,' she muttered in haste. 'So I reckoned you'd make the experience reasonably pleasant...and you *did*. Can we drop the subject now?'

Antonio might have dismissed that fantastic claim

had he not remembered her walking in to join him clad only in a towel and then virtually luring him down into the cushions. Scorching golden eyes lit on her like lightning bolts. 'You selected me like some kind of stud to have sex with you?'

'Look, least said, soonest mended,' Sophie mumbled, hot-cheeked, while wishing that she had come up with a less inflammatory story.

In a towering rage, Antonio sprang out of bed and began to get dressed at speed.

The intense claustrophobic silence intimidated and frightened Sophie.

'Antonio—?'

'Silencio!' His tone of derisive distaste sliced back at her, his lean, darkly handsome face grim. 'I had begun to think of you as my wife. *Qué risa*…what a laugh! I won't make that mistake again. I may have misjudged you the night after your sister's wedding, but you think like a slut and behave like one. It will be a cold day in hell before I share a bed with you again!'

All the colour bled from Sophie's heart-shaped face. 'Don't be like that. Stop being so angry with me—'

'What else did you expect? Approval?' Antonio dealt her a chilling appraisal. 'Your standards are not mine. From now on, we stick to the deal we agreed.'

Her hands were shaking. She had really offended him. She spun away so that he could no longer see her shaken face. Her eyes were hot and scratchy with tears and she was stiff with shock. It was better this way, she told herself wretchedly. They should not have gone to bed together. She should have had more self-control. Almost three years back she had listened to Pablo talking enviously at his own wedding about his older brother's phenomenal success with women. Naturally the act of sex would be a minor event to a guy like Antonio. Women were too easily available to him and who valued what was not in short supply? But what she could not bear was that Antonio should be so angry with her that he thought badly of her and condemned her for thinking like a slut.

She locked herself in the bathroom and studied herself with tear-filled eyes of pain and regret. If only the dream could have lasted a little longer, if only she had not settled on that stupid, shameless story of having slept with him purely to get rid of her virginity. Why had he believed that? Didn't he know how irresistible she found him? But when and how had she forgotten that he had only married her in the first place so that she could take care of Lydia? She had promised to leave him free to live exactly as he pleased. That recollection suddenly became the source of deep distress.

After a very poor night's sleep, Sophie got up soon after seven the next morning: Lydia would be awake and looking for her. She was really disconcerted to find Antonio in the nursery. He had Lydia in his arms and he was talking to her in soft Spanish.

Sophie hovered, determined to take the opportunity to clear the air between them. 'I wasn't expecting to find you in here.'

His keen dark-as-midnight eyes were level, his lean bronzed features unreadable. 'I thought I ought to say goodbye to Lydia—'

'Goodbye…you're going somewhere?' Sophie interrupted in dismay. 'Thanks for not waking me!'

The instant she made that crack she regretted it, for even to her own ears it sounded juvenile.

'I saw no reason to disturb you this early. I intended to phone later,' Antonio imparted with unassailable assurance. 'I have business to take care of. I had hoped to take a couple of days off and remain here, but it is not to be.'

Sophie had become very pale and tense. 'When will you be back?'

'I'm not quite sure,' he admitted calmly. 'I'm flying to Japan and then on to New York. After that, I must attend to matters in Madrid.'

'Antonio…' Hurt and disappointment and frustration were roaring through Sophie's slight frame. 'Don't you think we should talk?'

'I think that all that needed to be said was said last night,' Antonio countered with chillingly courteous finality.

Pride and intense insecurity silenced the apologetic tale of woe and explanation on Sophie's lips. She had met with rejection and disillusionment too often in life to deliberately court them. Why had she assumed that he would even be interested in what she had to say? After all, she was not an important element in Antonio's exclusive world. Why risk exposing herself to more of his contempt? If he was still angry with her, she reasoned unhappily, maybe it was better to let the dust settle for a couple of weeks before tackling him again.

'*Buenos días*, Sophie.' Doña Ernesta walked out onto the shaded upstairs loggia where Sophie was sewing while Lydia played on a rug at her feet. 'You must be the most industrious bride ever to enter this family. You are always at work.'

'But this isn't work…it's enjoyment.' As she placed a stitch in the fabric stretched over her embroidery frame Sophie glanced up. 'I'm not used to being lazy.'

'May I see your embroidery?'

Sophie obliged.

The old lady sighed in admiration over the intricate stitches and the fluid pattern of leaves and birds. 'You must know that this is work of an exceptional standard. You are extremely talented. Who taught you? Was it your mother?'

'I never knew my mother. It was a neighbour I used to visit as a child.' Sophie's eyes clouded with sadness as she remembered the elderly woman who had given her a much needed creative outlet. The chance to escape the noisy chaos of her father's home and visit, however briefly, a peaceful, organised household had been equally welcome. 'She taught me to sew when I was four years old and I was still learning from her ten years later when she died.'

'You must have been a rewarding pupil. Perhaps some day you will consider taking a textile conservation course.' Doña Ernesta lifted Lydia up onto her lap, smiling down at her great granddaughter with unconcealed pleasure. 'There are many very old pieces of needlework here which would benefit from your attention.'

'Even if I did a course, I don't think Antonio would want me touching family heirlooms,' Sophie muttered awkwardly.

Her companion regarded her in surprise. 'But you are a part of this family now.'

A maid arrived with a tray. 'I asked for English tea,' Doña Ernesta confided. 'And scones.'

At the old lady's request, Sophie poured the tea into fine china cups. Over the past week an increasing number of Antonio's relations and neighbours had made formal visits to meet Sophie and Doña Ernesta had been very supportive. Indeed the older woman was clearly intent on getting to know her grandson's wife. Sophie felt guilty that her own unhappiness was making it hard for her to respond with greater cheer to Doña Ernesta's more forthcoming manner.

'Have you heard from Antonio?' Doña Ernesta enquired gently.

Feeling very vulnerable, Sophie reddened. 'No…not for a couple of days.'

'He must be exceptionally busy,' Doña Ernesta immediately assured her in a soothing manner.

But with whom was Antonio busy? Sophie wondered wretchedly before she could suppress that unproductive thought. What was the point of tormenting herself? She had no control over what Antonio did. The sick sense of misery that she had been struggling to suppress threatened to rise up and overpower her. It was no comfort to know that her own hasty words had destroyed the fragile new relationship developing between her and Antonio. It was eight days since he had left the *castillo*. Although he had phoned several times the conversations had been brief and any attempt to stray into more intimate areas had been mercilessly snubbed.

'Sophie…may I speak freely to you?' Doña Ernesta asked then.

Sophie tensed. 'Of course…'

'You seem unhappy. I have no wish to pry,' the old lady assured her anxiously, 'but is there anything wrong?'

Sophie made a harried attempt to mount the cover-up that she knew Antonio would expect from her. 'Of course, there's nothing wrong.'

'It is natural that you should miss Antonio and very sad that you should be parted so soon after your wedding.'

Tears stung the back of Sophie's eyes in a dismaying

surge. It had not occurred to her that she would miss Antonio quite so dreadfully. But admitting even to herself that she had fallen very deeply in love with Antonio almost three years earlier and that indeed she had never got over him had destroyed all her natural defences.

'It is too dull here for you when he is away,' Doña Ernesta opined. 'Why don't you stay at our house in Madrid for a few days? You could shop and mix with the other young people in the family there. I believe you met some of them at your sister's wedding.'

Sophie was disconcerted by that suggestion but immediately aware of its appeal. Sitting around doing nothing was draining her confidence and depressing her. But if she went to Madrid without Antonio having first invited her there, it might look as if she were chasing after him. He might also be annoyed. The terms of their marriage deal did not allow her much room for independent manoeuvre, she reminded herself unhappily.

Whether she liked it or not, she had agreed that Antonio could do as he liked. All she had asked for in return was the right to care for Lydia and she had received that. In fact in material terms she really was doing very nicely indeed out of their marital agreement. She had Lydia and she was living in luxury. To top it all, in spite of her worst fears, even Antonio's grandmother was being really kind to her. So, really, she castigated herself, from where did she get the nerve to imagine that she had grounds for complaint?

On the other hand, hadn't the wedding night she had shared with Antonio blown that original agreement of theirs right out of the water? Everything felt so incredibly personal now. By making love to her, Antonio had turned their platonic relationship inside out. Everything had changed and that was his fault as much as hers.

Obviously she felt differently about him now and the chasm that had opened up between them truly frightened her. Overnight Antonio had become chillingly polite and unapproachable. The misunderstanding between them had to be sorted out, she reflected worriedly.

She decided that it would be best if she arrived in Madrid while Antonio was still abroad on business. That way her presence might look coincidental and he would not even need to know that he was being chased. If he were to ask her what she was doing there she would be able to say quite truthfully that neither she nor Lydia had anything to wear. Before the wedding, she had been too scared to spend his money on anything other than absolute necessities. Now, however, she was aware that Antonio was accustomed to perfectly groomed women. So, she too would get groomed to within an inch of her life. The hair, the nails, the cosmetics, the waxing, the whatever—she would go for the entire package. There was, Sophie acknowledged shamefacedly, very little she wouldn't do to get close to Antonio again. And if she failed, well, it wouldn't be for want of trying. After all, what did she have to lose?

Striding through Barajas airport, Antonio checked his watch with rare impatience. He would be at his Madrid home within the hour. It was almost three weeks since he had left the *castillo* and he was eager to see Sophie.

Not only to *see* her, his more honest self acknowledged, and a slightly rueful smile curved his handsome mouth. He could not understand how he had managed to make such a mess of things with her. Everything he had done had been out of character. But then he could never remember getting quite so angry with a woman before. The brooding bitterness of spirit that had followed had been equally new to his experience and profoundly disturbing for a male who prided himself on his self-discipline. He was neither moody, nor bad-tempered, and he was not one to hold a grudge. In short, his was not a volatile temperament and yet how else could he explain the explosive nature of his own behaviour on their wedding day?

With his customary cool logic restored he knew that Sophie's declaration that she had chosen him to be her stud was ridiculous. In a normal frame of mind he would have laughed that insult off. That had been Sophie putting him in his place. What had happened to his sense of humour that night and over the subsequent days when he had still seethed to such an extent that even speaking to her on the phone had been a challenge for him? Where had his even temper and his shrewd ability to read a situation gone? *Dios mio*, how could he have believed that nonsensical claim for longer than thirty seconds?

The knowledge that Sophie was in Madrid had increased his keenness to get home. It had been six days since he had even contrived to speak to her. He had been working very long hours and the time difference had forced him to phone at awkward times. Then, when he had called, Sophie had always been out. He assumed his grandmother was trotting Sophie and Lydia out to meet every friend and distant relative they possessed.

His chauffeur was so intent on the colourful celebrity magazine he was reading that he did not notice his employer's approach until the last possible moment, Antonio noted in some exasperation. Muttering embarrassed apologies, the older man rushed to open the passenger door and dropped the magazine. On the front cover it carried a picture of Sophie in the floral dress she had worn for their wedding. Antonio snatched it up in disbelief.

An article several pages long liberally spattered with photos of his wife greeted Antonio's incredulous gaze. The dress he had hated was rated as the cutting edge of true bridal style. There was Sophie looking improbably demure and dignified seated in the salon of his house in Madrid. She had let cameras into one of his homes! He breathed in very deep. There was Sophie prancing along a catwalk arm in arm with his cousin, Reina, at some charity fashion show…Sophie arriving at the opening night of a musical wearing a glittering red evening dress that fitted like a mermaid skin…Sophie showing the most shocking length of leg in a striped pink miniskirt as she climbed out of a Ferrari. *Whose* Ferrari? *Whose bloody Ferrari?*

He phoned his city home and learned that Sophie was out. He asked where she was and a hip nightclub was entioned as a possibility. He directed his chauffeur there instead and called his grandmother to ask her why he hadn't been informed that his wife was in town alone.

'Does Sophie need permission?' Doña Ernesta enquired.

'No. However, I understood that you were here with her.'

'Only for the first two days. Madrid exhausts me and Sophie makes friends so easily. She's an original and she has a great sense of style.'

Antonio replaced the phone with a strong sense of dissatisfaction. He began to read the gushing text in the article in the hope of finding out whom the Ferrari belonged to as well as an explanation for his wife's presence in it.

'Your Excellency...when you are finished, could I have the magazine back?' his chauffeur asked apologetically. 'My wife is keeping a scrapbook on the marquesa. You must be so proud of her. So much beauty and life!'

Sophie smiled when Reina's friend, Josias, urged her back onto the floor to dance and resisted the temptation to check her watch.

Whatever time it was scarcely mattered. By now, Antonio had to be back from the airport. She was proud that she had respected the rules that he had laid down at the outset of their marriage. She had done nothing to embarrass herself. Although she was absolutely desperate to see Antonio again, she had been strong. She had neither surrendered to her overpowering desire to rush to the airport to welcome him home, nor stayed in eagerly awaiting her lord and master's return.

From his stance at the top of the steps that led down onto the dance floor, Antonio scanned the crowds for Sophie. When he saw her, his intent gaze narrowed. Her dress bared her slender back and arms and slim, shapely legs. The fine fabric that clung to her delicate curves was the colour of polished pewter and it glistened below the lights as she spun, her mane of hair rippling round her. She was laughing as she danced and the young dark male smiling down at her was...Josias Marcaida, son of one of Antonio's biggest business rivals. A shark circling Sophie could not have filled Antonio with greater disquiet. He took the steps two at a time and forged a direct path across the floor to intercept the couple.

Sophie was enjoying the music and then she saw Antonio and froze. His commanding height and superb carriage brought him maximum attention. As she focused on his dark, lethally handsome features her awareness of everything else external fell away. She met scorching dark golden eyes and her tummy flipped as though she were being spun on a giant wheel. Suddenly she could hardly catch her breath and her pulses were racing. Anticipation held her so taut that she tingled and a little twist of heat flared in her pelvis.

Antonio closed one lean brown hand over hers. 'Tell Josias goodbye, *querida*,' he told her huskily as the thunder of the music quietened down for the DJ to talk.

Every nerve in her body was leaping and jumping like a soldier on parade. He had come to find her. Had he climbed Everest for her, she could not have been more thrilled.

'I have to go…' she framed dizzily in the general direction of her dance partner.

CHAPTER EIGHT

ANTONIO curved a powerful arm to Sophie's spine to urge her in the direction of the exit. She was almost there before it occurred to her that she could hardly leave without telling his cousin, Reina. Although the two women had not known each other long, they got on so well that Sophie already thought of Reina as a close friend.

'I have to tell Reina that I'm going—'

'You can phone my cousin from the limo—she'll understand.'

'No, that wouldn't be right. Just give me two minutes,' Sophie pleaded, pulling free to hurry back to the table where Reina was seated.

'Sorry, but I have to leave—'

'I saw Antonio arriving,' the elegant brunette acknowledged wryly.

Sophie gave her a relieved smile, for she had few secrets from Antonio's cousin. It was largely thanks to Reina, an up-and-coming fashion designer, that Sophie had managed to get to know so many people and step straight into a busy social life. She sped back to Antonio's side, but the wry quality of her friend's farewell had dented her buoyant mood. Although she was still intoxicated to be with Antonio again, Reina's noncommittal reaction had left her wondering if she should have responded with greater cool to Antonio's arrival.

Inside the limousine, Antonio reached for her with both hands. She had no thought of resisting him. Indeed a delicious little shiver of expectancy ran through her and her breath caught in her throat.

'Kiss me…' she whispered shakily.

Antonio did not get up close and personal in limos. He gazed down at her rapt face. Her amazingly green eyes clung to his. The ripe pout of her peach-tinted lips was pure, tantalising invitation.

'Antonio…' Sophie linked her arms round his neck.

Without any warning at all, Antonio found himself mentally picturing her spread half naked across the leather seat. His arousal was immediate and almost insufferably strong and all restraint vanished. Framing her cheekbones with spread fingers, he captured her mouth with hard, hungry intensity and his tongue delved deep.

He might as well have pressed a button and set Sophie on fire. Her entire body burned and she responded to that sensual assault with helpless enthusiasm.

Breathing raggedly, Antonio exerted every atom of control he could muster and dragged himself back from the brink of trying to live the fantasy pictures playing out inside his head. 'Let's chill until we get home…'

Belatedly conscious that the chauffeur could see them, Sophie reddened with embarrassment. She had grabbed Antonio. Why had she done that? She wanted to cringe and die there and then. Did she never learn? Why was she continually tempted to make a fool of herself around him?

Antonio dragged in a steadying breath and decided that if he talked, he would manage to keep his hands off her long enough to get home. 'You look amazing in that dress.'

Any desire to play it cool left Sophie at spectacular

speed and her soft mouth stretched into a huge smile. 'Thank you…'

'But…' Antonio intertwined his fingers with hers again and paused for a second, lean dark features reflective '…I have to admit that I also think the dress is too revealing for my wife to wear.'

'Oh…' Sophie framed in dismay and surprise at that unexpected criticism. 'But it's not that short and it's not see-through or anything like that.'

'It attracts too much attention, *mi rica*,' Antonio informed her gravely. 'A lot of men were staring at you.'

Sophie blinked and hurriedly dropped her lashes before he could read her expression. But she almost burst out laughing. He was so deadly serious. Men had been looking at her and therefore her clothing had to be at fault. 'Maybe they just thought I was pretty,' she dared to suggest.

'Whatever…I don't like it when other men watch you in that way,' Antonio affirmed without hesitation.

It was like the sun was rising inside Sophie and she was trying to contain the wonderful golden heat of its rays, for, unless she was very much mistaken, Antonio was jealous of other guys so much as looking at her!

'In point of fact,' Antonio continued, retaining a hold on her hand, 'it's not a good idea for you to be at a nightclub with a crowd of singles.'

Her fine brows drew together, for she was mystified by that statement. 'Why not?'

'Josias Marcaida is a womaniser—'

'Oh, I know that,' Sophie broke in. 'Reina warned me, but she also said that Josias wasn't a patch on you!'

Antonio stiffened at that unwelcome response. 'I do not think you should be discussing me with other family members.'

Her expressive mouth tightening, Sophie tugged her hand free of his. 'Right…so you don't like the dress, don't like me talking to your relations, don't like me going out to a club—'

'I think what I'm trying to say,' Antonio delivered smooth as silk and in no way apologetically, 'could be summed up in one sentence.'

'So say the magic sentence and save time,' Sophie advised curtly, temper licking up inside her in little orange flames hungry for sustenance. As she turned her head sharply away she realised the limo was already coming to a halt outside the hugely imposing dwelling that was the Rocha family home in Madrid.

'You're no longer single…you're my wife.'

Sophie breathed in so deep she honestly thought her lungs might burst. But the deep breathing helped her to emerge from the car, climb the steps with a fixed smile on her lips for the benefit of the hovering housekeeper and head straight for the stairs.

'Sophie…?' Antonio questioned with calm authority.

Sophie spun on the stairs, treated Antonio to a look that should have sent him up in flames and murmured tight and low, 'One more word and I'll be up for murder…'

'I've said nothing to which you should take exception,' Antonio countered, beautiful dark golden eyes daring her to argue.

'You…total hypocrite,' Sophie whispered, green eyes wild with raging reproach.

'Spain is civilising you, *querida*,' Antonio responded in retaliation, for he felt that he had been extremely tolerant and understanding. After all, he had found his provocatively dressed wife dancing the night away in a nightclub with a notorious playboy. 'A month ago you would have shouted that at the top of your voice and you wouldn't have cared who heard you.'

It was an unfortunate remark. Her jewel-bright eyes raked over him in a tempestuous surge.

'You may not be very tall...but in your own special way, you're quite magnificent,' Antonio remarked, his brilliant gaze welded to her with raw appreciation. He mounted the stairs with the subtle predatory grace of a big game hunter closing in on a target. 'I missed you.'

'I don't care!' Sophie launched back down at him even though she knew she did care very much and her angry voice echoed round the landing like a crash of feminine thunder. 'It's at times like this that I hate you!'

Having flung that declaration, Sophie headed with fast and furious steps for the sanctuary of her bedroom. She wanted to punch something. She really wanted to punch him, but he was off limits because she would not have liked it had he punched her. How dared he remind her that she was his wife in that superior tone of censure? How dared he even refer to her with that label?

Antonio strode into her room only a split second in her wake. 'You don't hate me,' he told her with infuriating confidence.

'We had an agreement and you made that agreement. You told me that you wanted to hang onto your freedom!'

Antonio lifted and dropped a broad shoulder in fatalistic style. 'I'm not denying it.'

'And then out of the blue you show up and you start telling me that I have to behave like a *real* wife!'

'But you *are* a real wife,' Antonio asserted.

'Maybe technically speaking...but that angle doesn't matter,' Sophie told him heatedly. 'We need to talk about you practising what you preach.'

Antonio was fascinated by the way she was laying down the law. She employed neither flattery nor feminine guile to state her case. She was not afraid to say exactly what she thought. But no woman had ever utilised such a direct approach on Antonio and he was impressed. 'Is that a fact?'

'Yes, it is,' Sophie confirmed with vehemence, her heart-shaped face flushed with anger. 'You said you wanted your freedom but that means…that *has* to mean that you're not entitled to interfere with mine…right?'

'Wrong. *En realidad*…you are very wrong on that score,' Antonio declared, lean, powerful face taut. 'Tonight I could not even stand by and watch you dance with another man without feeling that something was wrong.'

Sophie's eyes opened to their fullest extent. 'I can't believe I'm hearing this.'

'You're my wife. You wear my ring on your finger. You live in my home. You cannot be my wife and independent of me—'

Her hands knotted into fists, Sophie argued, 'Oh, yes, I can be!'

'It is a contradiction in terms—'

'Like husband and free agent?' Sophie fenced back with saccharine sweetness.

'A good comparison. But every time you shout at me, I feel married, *querida*,' Antonio confided with a glint of raw mockery in his golden gaze.

Incensed by his levity, Sophie treated him to an unamused appraisal. He need not think that she was about to be swayed by the simple fact that he was an outrageously good-looking guy with a killer smile. 'Obviously a lot of women have let you away with this sort of nonsense, but I won't let you away with anything,' Sophie warned him. 'There is no way I will ever accept this one-rule-for-you-and-another-rule-for-me attitude—'

'But that is not what I advocate.'

'But that's exactly what you're advocating…' She stumbled over that unfamiliar word and in the interim he pronounced it correctly for her. A sense of humiliation stormed through her anger and brought hot tears to her eyes. 'That's what I mean about you…you're impossible. You are Spanish and you're correcting my English!'

'That was thoughtless,' Antonio acknowledged.

'No, it wasn't. You think about everything, you always know exactly what you're doing—'

'I *didn't* know exactly what I was doing when I married you. I didn't look for the bigger picture. I must have been insane; I was certainly guilty of poor judgement,' Antonio countered grimly. 'I did not even foresee the complications that would arise from the consummation of our marriage. But from that night, my desire for freedom was inequitable and unrealistic.'

A pounding silence had fallen. Sophie was listening to his every word and she was trembling. 'As far as I'm concerned you can forget about what happened on our wedding night. You wanted to keep your freedom and you can still do that!' she told him boldly. 'You don't owe me anything and, if you stay away from me from now on, we can go right back to that agreement we made. All we need to do is be sensible from now on and we'll soon forget that we ever strayed from the deal.'

His dark golden eyes flared bright as sunlight at that frank proposition. He held her strained gaze levelly.

'That's a very generous offer in the circumstances. But there's a problem—'

'Nothing's perfect, Antonio!' Sophie riposted fiercely, because her heart felt as if it were breaking inside her. It had cost her a lot to make that generous offer. In truth she could have happily chained him to her bed.

'I know, but I can't forget our wedding night and I can't stay away from you either. I suspect that being "sensible" might well be beyond my power at present.'

Utterly unprepared for that statement and thrown into a loop by it, Sophie stared at him in confusion. 'Sorry?'

'You're incredibly tempting. I'm very attracted to you. I fought it every minute of the day the whole time I was away from you, *querida*,' Antonio heard himself admit harshly, for the knowledge that he had lost that battle still rankled like salt in a wound. 'That attraction is not sensible and it's not the deal we agreed either. But, right now, I don't want to be with any other woman; I want to be with you.'

'But...but that's not how it's supposed to be,' Sophie mumbled in shock.

'That is how it *has* to be,' Antonio affirmed, his strong jaw line squaring. 'We should forget how it was supposed to be. I can't stand back and watch you enjoy the same freedom that I once intended to take for myself. For now, let's enjoy being married.'

Sophie was no fool. There was a big smile trying to break out across her lips, for he was offering her a lifeline but she had picked up on his every qualification as well. *Right now...I want to be with you.* He was already accepting that there would be a time when he no longer wanted her. *For now, let's enjoy being married.* Again, a suggestion rooted very much in the present without any reference to the future. He was not suggesting that their marriage become a proper marriage, not really he wasn't, she reasoned painfully. What Antonio was really proposing was that they treat their marriage as if it were an affair. Basically, if she stripped everything he had said bare and got down to the basics, all he was offering her was fidelity in the short term and sex.

'Tonight, I would have liked you to meet me at the airport,' Antonio admitted so that she would know the next time. 'When you weren't there, I was determined not to come back here without you. Perhaps only then was I allowing myself to admit how much I had been looking forward to seeing you.'

As though drawn by an invisible magnet, Sophie was moving closer to him with slow, tentative steps. To the conditions of fidelity and sex, she was adding in airport meetings and thinking that that latter request was rather sweet and unexpected. 'I've hardly even spoken to you since you went away—'

'You avoided my calls—'

She coloured because it was true. 'Yeah…but you were very cold on the phone—'

'I was at war with myself, *querida*. I'm not now and I will never be again,' Antonio promised huskily.

Sophie felt light-headed with relief. She reckoned that she could probably drown and die happy in his gorgeous eyes. Nothing lasted for ever, she reminded herself dizzily. Life offered no certainties. But she loved Antonio and she was ready to take what she could have rather than hang out for what she could not. He was never going to ask her to stay married to him for good. He wasn't in love with her. He was in lust with her.

But then they could never have had a future together anyway, she reflected with a stab of pained regret. He didn't know it and she saw no reason why she should ever tell him, but she was all too wretchedly aware that she was unlikely to ever be able to have a baby. And there he was with his title, his ancestral castle and centuries of family history. He might not be that keen to tie himself down for ever yet, but some day Antonio would be very keen to hand on that title and that rich and ancient heritage to a child of his own. Understandably he would want a wife who could give him children in his future. A future in which she could not and would not feature.

Far from impervious to the distanced look that had darkened her gaze, Antonio eased her up against his lean, powerful frame with the sure hands of a male to whom sensuality was an art. 'You look unhappy,' he murmured.

'I'm not...I'm not,' Sophie insisted, stretching up to tug loose his tie and unbutton his collar.

Refusing to be distracted, he caught her active fingers up in his, turned up her palm and pressed his mouth there for a moment. He glanced back up at her heart-shaped face to see if her eyes still held that same poignant look of sorrow. 'Why are you sad?'

'It's a secret...nothing you'd be interested in—'

'Try me,' Antonio urged, for the instant she mentioned that fatal word, the instant she admitted that she was holding back something from him, he was on fire with the need to know what the secret encompassed.

'No, some things are private,' she whispered ruefully, letting a questing fingertip rub along the hard, masculine angularity of his jaw line. A faint dark bluish shadow of stubble roughened his bronzed skin and somehow made his beautiful, sensual mouth seem even more appealing, she reflected dizzily.

Antonio lowered his arrogant dark head and let the tip of his tongue flick the swollen pinkness of her lower lip. She gasped at his touch and her legs wobbled. 'If the secret relates to a problem there is a very good chance that I could sort it out for you,' he intoned gravely.

Sophie squeezed her eyes tight shut to rein back the stinging surge of tears his offer had unleashed. She loved his pride and his confidence and his immediate conviction that he could come up with a cure for everything short of death. Not to mention his very traditional assumption that it was somehow his duty and responsibility to deal with anything that worried her. 'Not this particular one,' she told him gruffly.

'Trust me…' But even as he said it he was wondering if her secret related to her inability to have children. He did not want to think about that. Never before had he experienced that reluctance to consider an issue. But he discovered that he did not even want to think about *why* that particular issue was such a hotbed of sensitivity even for him.

'No…' Her voice was muffled because she was pushing her tear-wet face into his shirtfront and fighting to get a grip on her strong emotions.

There was no need for him to know that she was barren, no need at all. Who could tell how he would react? She could not bear the idea of him pitying her. Even worse, he might begin viewing her as flawed, less of a woman and not quite so attractive. She had learned that, without really thinking about it, people tended to associate fertility with all sorts of other feminine attributes.

'Some day you *will* trust me, *gatita*,' Antonio swore with fervour and, closing his arms round her, he lifted her right off her feet. He crushed her to his hard, muscular chest and sealed his mouth to hers in a passionate, drugging kiss. Her ribs complained and oxygen was in short supply, but she loved that enthusiastic demonstration of all-male strength and protectiveness.

With immense care he laid her down on the bed and then cast off his jacket and tie where he stood.

'There really hasn't been anyone since…?' Sophie prompted shyly.

He ripped off the shirt without ceremony and smiled down at her. 'For the first time in my adult life, I've lived like a celibate.'

Sophie kicked off her shoes and lay back against the pillows like an old-style temptress, back arched, bosom prominent, knees slightly raised to display her legs to their best advantage.

'You've been practising the seduction pose,' Antonio breathed with amusement.

Sophie shifted a narrow shoulder in a languid movement to let the strap of her dress slide down, allowing just the hint of a pouting breast to be seen.

'And the effort has paid off,' Antonio conceded in another tone entirely, much impressed until he was assailed by an uneasy suspicion. 'You haven't been doing this for any other guy…have you?'

Sophie shot him a shocked look. 'Of course not…I've been behaving myself too!'

Antonio breathed again. 'I should have flown back and sorted this out more than a week ago.'

'Maybe you weren't ready.'

Antonio was still not sure that he was ready for the enormous complexity that had disrupted his once smooth and calm existence. He had not chosen the situation, but now at least he felt in control of it again.

He surveyed Sophie with unashamed masculine possessiveness. He could not comprehend how he had ever dismissed her as only very pretty. Her slanting cheekbones were distinctive and her clear bright eyes were beautiful and her skin had the creamy bloom of perfection.

'Why are you staring at me?' Sophie whispered anxiously.

'I like looking at you, *querida*,' Antonio murmured thickly, sinking down on the edge of the bed and lifting her on to his powerful thighs.

A tiny shiver ran through her as he undid the tiny hooks holding up the delicate bodice of her dress. He brushed the fragile fabric out of his path and discovered that she was not wearing a bra. Her face flamed and she stopped breathing altogether, madly conscious of the jutting swell of her bare breasts and the straining prominence of her rosy nipples.

'You are perfect,' Antonio groaned, bending her back over a strong arm and letting his hungry mouth roam over her tender flesh with a skill that wrenched shaken little cries of helpless response from her. 'The entire time I've been away I've been thinking about making love to you…I've hardly slept for wanting you.'

'I dream about you,' she muttered feverishly.

Antonio stood her up between his spread thighs and sent the dress skimming down to her feet. He hooked a finger into her pale pink panties and sent them travelling in the same direction. Wide-eyed, she stared at him, her face hot. Scorching golden eyes melded to hers, he nudged her thighs apart and explored the warm, damp entrance below the caramel curls crowning her feminine mound. A fiery, raging ache stirred low in her belly.

Excitement clenched every muscle in her body and her legs shook.

'You're ready for me, *enamorada*,' Antonio husked with raw, masculine satisfaction.

He swept her up and tumbled her down again on the foot of the bed. Her heart was pumping fast; she was quivering, unable to stay still. Her body was super sensitive and burning up with painful longing. He was magnificently aroused and he plunged his hot, hard heat into the tight, tender core between her legs. She lifted up to him in a torment of wild pleasure. Then nothing existed for her but his passionate dominance and the frenzied climb to the peak of ecstasy. He drove her out of control and inhibition into a world of voluptuous abandonment. She clung to him as the sweet convulsions of heart-stopping excitement claimed her and released her from her own body in an intoxicating explosion of sensation.

'Don't even think of going to sleep, *querida*,' Antonio warned her, pinning her flat under him to capture her reddened lips in a sensually savage kiss.

Sophie gave him a dazed smile. Her body was still humming and purring with wicked little after-quakes of pure pleasure. It was amazing how the mechanics of actual sex had once struck her as being the most ridiculous arrangement ever. Yet when Antonio got passionate, she felt as if intimacy was the most wondrous joy ever and a positive passport to paradise. She linked her arms round him, breathed in the thrilling scent of his damp bronzed skin and marvelled at the feeling that he had been invented and indeed created solely for her benefit.

'You're fantastic,' he drawled, holding her close. 'And the best thing of all is that you're mine.'

'For a while,' she qualified without even thinking, needing simply to remind herself of that reality.

His lithe, strong body tensed from head to toe. 'It could be for a very long while.'

Sadly, Sophie did not think it would be. She did not feel that she would hold his attention that long. Eventually his craving for freedom would surface again. Then he would be grateful that he wasn't in a normal marriage and tied down to a wife and children… Her thoughts switched course at that point. Her smooth brow indented as she realised that on neither occasion on which they had shared a bed had Antonio made use of any protection. She was astonished that he had been so careless. My goodness, had he assumed that she was on the contraceptive pill?

She lifted her head, but not high enough to meet his eyes. 'You haven't taken any precautions…er, you know, in case of pregnancy,' she muttered awkwardly.

Suddenly Antonio was very still and calling himself a fool, for that oversight might well have betrayed his knowledge of her condition. He did not want to distress her by admitting the truth. 'My mistake…I thought perhaps you might have taken care of that.'

'No.' Relaxing again, she nestled her head back in below his shoulder.

'I promise that I'll be more careful from now on,' Antonio swore and his arms tightened round her. He smoothed a soothing hand down over her tumbled curls until the tension had left her small, slight frame and pressed his mouth to the tiny vivid butterfly tattooed on her shoulder.

But Sophie could not get over how careless he had been. Then she thought of all the babies born to men who seemed to want nothing to do with them and decided that such recklessness was possibly a common male trait. Was there even the slightest possibility that she might conceive? For the first time in her life she allowed herself the indulgence of toying with that unlikely prospect. When she was twelve years old, her father had told her that the doctor had thought it was doubtful that she would ever have kids of her own.

'Isn't there even a chance?' she had asked then.

'Yeah, he said there's always a chance, but not much of one. Why are you worrying about it? Kids spoil your life. You'll be better off without them.'

So maybe there was a one-in-ten-million chance that a miracle might occur and she would conceive. Why was she even thinking such nonsense? Antonio, she thought painfully, would be absolutely appalled if she were to fall pregnant. He would already have an image of the kind of woman he would choose to become the mother of his child. She was willing to bet that the likely lady would be blue-blooded, beautiful and fancy just as he was. But that woman would still be only his *second* wife. Well, at least she'd have been the first wife and nobody could take that away from her, Sophie reminded herself dully. Although she had to remember that she was only a wife because of Lydia and only in bed with Antonio because he had an overactive libido. Wasn't that the most likely explanation of all?

'I've arranged to take a couple of weeks off,' Antonio confessed, striving for a casual note. 'I need to spend more time with you and Lydia.'

Sophie splayed small fingers across the hair-roughened expanse of his virile chest and released a contented sigh. 'You definitely do.'

He rolled over, swinging her under him to gaze down at her with smouldering dark golden eyes. 'Do you think you could keep me entertained for that length of time?'

'I'm not sure.' Sophie surveyed his lean bronzed face from beneath her curling lashes, a newly playful light in her sparkling gaze. 'After all, the boot will be on the other foot.'

'Meaning?'

'Josias might be a tough act for you to follow.'

Reluctant appreciation of that sally lit Antonio's appraisal even as his big, powerful body tensed at the impudence of that challenge and suggested comparison. 'Anything he can do…' Antonio shrugged with magnificent assurance. 'Can you doubt it, *gatita*?'

Her heart swelled with love, for his supreme confidence made her feel safe. 'I have no doubts about you at all—'

'That sounds ominous.' Antonio finally slotted in a question he had been holding back for quite a few minutes in search of the right light moment. 'I saw that interview you did with the magazine—'

'Wasn't it amazing? Didn't the cameraman make me look really special?' Sophie exclaimed with pleasure. 'I did it for a charity…you'd be amazed at the size of the donation the magazine made to their funds. The interviewer said really nice things about me too—'

'Journalists generally do in publications of that nature. If they were unpleasant, people would not give them access to their lives and their homes,' Antonio said drily.

'I never thought of that. But I was hoping you would see the interview and be proud of me. What did you think?' she prompted eagerly.

That, aside of the business news, a Rocha should only receive a mention in print on the occasions of birth, marriage and death. That was Antonio's attitude to all such publicity.

Antonio sidestepped the question. 'I wondered who the Ferrari in the photos belonged to—'

'Josias…'

Antonio was learning that the mere mention of a name could set his teeth on edge.

'He gave me a lift from Reina's apartment to a restaurant. Of course, if you take me out to eat at least once a week, promise to teach me how to drive and constantly tell me that I'm fantastically beautiful and fantastic fun, I could probably get by without Josias,' Sophie told him deadpan, dancing green eyes pinned to his frowning incredulity.

'Yes to the eating out. No to the driving— I'd be a hellish teacher. As for Josias's seduction routine, I don't copy,' Antonio informed her huskily, rearranging her under him to his own very precise requirements and with a sexual intimacy and finesse that made her shiver in wanton anticipation of the pleasure to come. 'I have my own methods, *mi rica*.'

But it was the smile that transfixed Sophie. That dazzling, charismatic smile that was purely for her and the conviction he gave that nothing was more important than her at that moment. It was her dream, and shutting out her misgivings and her fears, she surrendered to living her dream.

CHAPTER NINE

SIX weeks later, Sophie sat in the bright and colourful nursery watching Antonio demonstrate in all seriousness to Lydia how to crawl. Amusement was threatening to crack her up, but she managed to keep a straight face. All his life Antonio had been a high achiever and, having read a book on child development, he had learned all the important milestones and was keen to see Lydia sprint ahead of her peers.

'You're wasting your time,' Sophie warned him gently. 'Some babies may crawl at this age, but I don't think Lydia is likely to be one of them. She's too laid-back and contented to rush into making that much effort.'

'Perhaps all she needs is encouragement,' Antonio informed her stubbornly while his niece chuckled at the sight of him on hands and knees and held up her arms to be lifted.

'No, Lydia's not the physically active type. You can tell by the way she behaves. Belinda was like that. She loved to be lazy. I could hardly get her out of bed in the morning.'

'But her daughter just might take after my side of the family—'

'I think we'd know by now if that was on the cards,' Sophie interposed. 'We'd have found her barking out orders to the staff through the bars of her cot, setting her own developmental targets and threatening to leave home unless we let her sit up to watch the stock market close.'

A slow grin curved Antonio's handsome mouth. 'I don't bark out orders…'

'Well, you do it very politely, but you are an incredibly bossy person,' Sophie told him, watching him surrender to Lydia's pantomime of pathetic pleading and hoist his delighted niece in the air. 'Just promise me one thing…that you're not going to be disappointed with Lydia if she fails to set the world on fire.'

Antonio shot her a look of reproach. 'Of course not. As her parents we can hope and pray that she enjoys good health and happiness as she grows up. But beyond that her life will be what she chooses it to be.'

His common-sense outlook impressed Sophie and she scolded herself for worrying that he might have too high expectations of Lydia. After all, in recent weeks she had come to appreciate that Antonio was demonstrating all the signs of becoming a fantastic father. For a start, Lydia just adored him. Her little face shone with trust and love and pleasure the instant Antonio appeared. Antonio might have started out spending time with Lydia because he knew that that was what he ought to do. But his niece's enthusiastic response to his attention had swiftly won her his interest and affection for her own sake.

As for Sophie, she was simply basking in the kind of happiness she had never dared to hope might be hers. Six weeks ago, Antonio had swept her and Lydia off to a Caribbean villa for the best part of a month. They had had a wonderful time. He had taught her how to sail and swim and snorkel, and she had taught him how to make the sort of basic sandcastle that Lydia could then be allowed to destroy. Even with a baby in tow the number of staff looking after their needs had ensured that the holiday was a honeymoon in every sense of the word.

There had been long, endless days when they had barely stirred further than the sunlit privacy of the terrace beyond their bedroom. Days they had barely got out of bed and surrendered body and soul to the overwhelming magnetic attraction that kept on welding them back together again when satiation ought to have long since set in. She studied him with a secret smile. He was an incredible lover and in that department they appeared to be a perfect match. He might not be able to keep his hands off her, but she was equally useless at keeping her hands off him, she conceded with hot cheeks. Every time she saw him she wanted to connect with him in some way just to convince herself that he was still hers.

Since returning from the Caribbean they had spent most of their time at the *castillo*. There the more leisurely pace of life and the vast swathe of countryside encompassed by the Salazar estate allowed them a peaceful seclusion that they could have found in no other place. Sophie had got to know the staff, had managed to handle a couple of semi-formal dinner parties and was gradually becoming acquainted with the tenants as well. She now had quite a vocabulary of Spanish words and expressions and had agreed to teach new stitches to the needlework group that met in the village. Her skill with a needle had crossed the barriers of language and nationality and had done more than anything else to help her to win acceptance as Antonio's wife.

Antonio closed his arms round her as she straightened from settling Lydia into her cot. 'Lunch…' he growled soft and low.

The feel and the familiar scent of him hit Sophie like an instant aphrodisiac and she wriggled back shamelessly into the hard, muscular shelter of his lithe, powerful body.

'Keep on doing that and you're likely to go hungry until we dine this evening,' Antonio promised in a husky purr.

Her knees went weak at that sensual threat. She leant back into his impressively male frame, wickedly conscious of the helpless awakening of her own body. He used a certain tone of voice and looked at her with those spectacular golden eyes in a certain way and she just melted into a pitiful puddle of eager longing.

'I would rather have you than lunch…' she admitted, her cheeks warm with embarrassment over her own boldness.

With a throaty laugh of masculine appreciation at that frank confession, Antonio spun her round to face him. 'You must have been made specially for me, *enamorada*.'

'Or you must've been made for me,' Sophie traded.

In the corridor outside the nursery he dragged her into his arms and captured her mouth with a devastating urgency that left her dizzy. 'You've turned my life upside down,' he breathed raggedly. 'But I like it this way.'

His mobile phone started ringing before they even reached the bedroom. They exchanged mutually irritated glances and with a sigh he answered it. She knew by the shadowing of his lean dark features that something important had come up and that he would have to leave.

An estate tenant, an old man who had known Antonio from childhood, had been ill for a long time and was asking for him to visit.

'I must go and see him,' Antonio said gravely.

'I know.' Sophie masked her disappointment and smiled to show that she understood, for she had learned to appreciate his serious side and the strong sense of responsibility that drove him.

She opened the bedroom door and stared wide-eyed at the superb arrangements of white flowers that flourished in several corners. The air was heavy with the scent of blossom. 'My goodness...'

'It was supposed to be a surprise. I should have kept you out of this room until I got back,' Antonio groaned.

'My birthday's still a week away—'

'I know...' Antonio watched her remove the envelope from the biggest floral display. 'But we have now been together for two months and we're celebrating, *querida*.'

Her throat thickened and her eyes misted over with tears as she scrutinised the gift card. It was such a romantic gesture and she was really touched. What had happened to their marriage of convenience? He had said to forget how their marriage was supposed to be and she had needed no encouragement to forget that original businesslike agreement, for she was madly, hopelessly in love with him. He had suggested that they enjoy being married and since then every day, every night had been a joy for her. Nobody had ever made so much effort to bring her happiness. Was it any wonder that she simply adored him? With an unsteady hand she skated a fingertip over a delicate white blossom.

'You don't like them?'

Fiercely blinking back the moisture in her aching eyes, she flung her arms round him, hugged him tight and whispered gruffly, 'I love them, I really, really love them and appreciate the thought.'

Antonio drove out to the isolated farm to visit the old man, who had once been the estate farrier. He was taking his leave of the sick man's family early that evening when his phone rang again. It was his friend, Navarro Teruel, the family doctor.

'Could you come and see me at the surgery?' Navarro sounded unusually stilted. 'I know I usually come up to the castle, but on this occasion you might find my office more suitable.'

Climbing into the dusty four-wheel drive he used on the estate, Antonio frowned. 'I could come right now. Is there something wrong?'

'I'd prefer not to discuss this on the phone,' Navarro told him awkwardly.

Antonio dug his phone back in his pocket. He felt slightly nauseous. Was it his grandmother? Doña Ernesta had been pronounced fighting fit at a recent examination. But a couple of weeks earlier Antonio had allowed Navarro to run a full battery of tests, including DNA, on Lydia. *Dios mio!* Had that medical turned up a disease? But why had it taken so long for Navarro to approach him with the adverse result?

Sophie didn't even know about half those tests. Having arranged to take Lydia to Navarro for a vaccination that had been overdue, Sophie had come down with a twenty-four-hour virus that had confined her to bed and it had been Antonio who had taken the baby instead. Navarro had been very thorough. He had sympathised with Antonio's concern about the risk of a heart murmur and his friend's desire not to worry his wife unnecessarily. But in most cases heart murmurs could be dealt with, Antonio reminded himself. Why had Navarro sounded so bleak and constrained?

Antonio drove to the surgery with the immense care

of someone worried sick. What if there was something seriously wrong with Lydia? Leukaemia, he thought strickenly. Could it run in families? He pictured Lydia, who was the most cheerful baby imaginable, suffering and fighting for her life. His hands gripped the steering wheel with the fierce power of his disturbed emotions. He imagined what that terrible battle would do to Sophie…and to him. He knew that he would have to be strong for all of them. He knew that just at the moment he did not feel strong. He wanted to rage against fate with every atom of his being.

Navarro, a tall, thin, bespectacled man opened the door of the surgery. It was after opening hours and the reception area was empty and silent. 'Come in, Antonio.'

Lean, powerful face pale and grim, Antonio refused the offer of a seat. 'Just give me the bad news.'

'The DNA results on your late sister-in-law's child arrived this afternoon.'

'You invited me here to discuss that DNA stuff?' Antonio interrupted in surprise.

'You asked me to take care of the testing when you brought Lydia to see me,' Navarro reminded him. 'As you know I did the saliva tests on you and her and sent them off. I imagine that, like me, you thought no more of the matter.'

'I didn't…' Antonio agreed, endeavouring to rise above his concern for Lydia to absorb this new and unexpected information. 'I assumed that you had asked me here to tell me that there's something wrong with Lydia.'

'Lydia is a perfectly healthy child.' But Navarro was still frowning when he extended a folded sheet of paper to his former school friend. 'But you had better look at this. I dealt with the DNA testing personally, so none of my staff have had access to this information.'

Antonio flipped open the document and read the typed lines several times over with fierce concentration. 'This can't be true…there must be some mistake!' he contended in flat rebuttal.

'I'm sorry, but the tests prove beyond doubt that Lydia is not your brother's child,' Navarro pronounced with a regretful sigh. 'The child is not related to your family. She carries none of your genes.'

Antonio was so shocked he dropped heavily down onto the chair opposite the other man. He began to speak and then thought better of it. An intensely private man at the best of times, he immediately battened down the hatches of his reserve on his personal reactions. Navarro might be his oldest friend from childhood, but this was a family matter that touched his honour.

'I'm sure that this news will be equally distressing for your wife to hear, which is why I preferred not to come up to the castle. Try not to judge Lydia's mother too harshly, my friend…'

Antonio was no longer listening. Incredulous dark anger was rising in a flood tide inside him, washing away the trusting foundations of the newer ties that had formed in more recent times. The child he regarded as his niece, the baby he had learned to regard as his own daughter, was an impostor, a fake. She had not a drop of the blood of the Rocha family in her veins. Who had put forward Lydia's claim? Belinda—and through Belinda, Sophie. The sisters must both have known the truth. He refused to believe otherwise.

Antonio sprang upright. 'I must go home.'

Navarro looked concerned. 'Take some time to come

to terms with this, Antonio. People do make mistakes and often the innocent foot the price.'

But Antonio was too outraged to embrace such a philosophical view and too close to the sharp end to feel generous. He had allowed himself to become the victim of a scam! What else could it be? He had married a virtual stranger on the strength of his conviction that that little girl was his brother's child. But he should have insisted that DNA tests to prove the child's identity were done first. In retrospect he could not credit that he had been so gullible. He had actually ignored the legal advice he had received at the time. His own lawyer had advised caution and tests, but Antonio had been impatient to get the marriage over and done with and the situation resolved. He had also been ashamed of the part his dishonest brother had played in his late wife's impoverishment. Questioning the paternity of Belinda's child against such a background would have been adding insult to injury.

But wasn't it strange that just at the point when he had decided simply to remove Lydia from Sophie's care something had happened to change his mind? How much had he been influenced by Mrs Moore's well-timed sob story about Sophie's inability to have a baby of her own? Had Sophie even had leukaemia when she was a child? How did he know that she was infertile? That story had not come from Sophie personally and tact had prevented him from approaching her for verification. If Mrs Moore had lied to further Sophie's hope of enriching herself through Lydia, Sophie would be able to disclaim any responsibility for the fact.

Back at the *castillo*, Antonio strode into the vast and imposing salon and poured himself a brandy. As he replaced the stopper on the crystal decanter he noticed that his hand was unsteady. He drained the goblet and strode upstairs to the nursery. He did not know why his steps had automatically taken him up there. The room was dimly lit and the nanny, who was tidying away clothes, slipped away to leave him in peace with her charge.

Lydia was fast asleep, her little face serene below the mop of her curls. She looked very much like Sophie, he acknowledged. Lydia had the same delicate build, facial shape and creamy skin, but her hair was darker than her aunt's and her eyes a different colour. Antonio surveyed the child whom he now knew had nothing to do with him at all. Fierce bitterness laced his mood. He had never had much interest in children but he had still learned to love Lydia. Yet she was a stranger's child even if she did not feel like a stranger and was Sophie not a stranger too? After all, the woman he had believed her to be would never have deceived him in such a manner.

Sophie studied herself critically in the dressing room mirror and decided that she looked downright indecent. If the fire alarm went off and she was forced to jump from a window, she would have to pretend that the reason she was in her underclothes was that she was fresh out of her bath. She was wearing a lace-trimmed blue silk lingerie set adorned with tiny roses and seed pearls. On her terms the flimsy camisole and panties were the last word in erotic presentation and daring. Did she look daft? Women photographed in similar get-ups for magazines always had legs that went on for ever and beautiful faces stamped with superior expressions of extreme boredom. She practised looking bored while struggling to suppress her worst fear: suppose Antonio laughed?

The food she had ordered arrived on a trolley along with an ice bucket and champagne. Casting off her wrap again, she took the trolley into the bedroom and began lighting scented candles. He gave her flowers and a romantic card and she gave him…a rerun of their wedding night with supper on the floor and sex. She winced, green eyes reflecting her mortification over that analogy. Well, she couldn't tell him she loved him, could she? He certainly wouldn't thank her for any soppy confessions of that nature. *Let's enjoy being married,* he had said. There was nothing deep or emotional about that suggestion.

Nervously she fingered the glittering diamond pendant in the shape of a flower at her throat. He had given it to her while they were abroad. He had also bought her an exquisite watch and diamond-studded ear hoops and she had no doubt that she would receive something even more expensive and precious to mark her birthday. He had bought her and Lydia a host of other little gifts as well. He was very generous. Ought she just to have bought him something? No, she decided, when a guy could buy himself anything, a woman had to go that extra mile to make an impression. But did she look cheap…sluttish?

When the door opened, she called out, 'Antonio? Close your eyes before you come in!'

He didn't close his eyes: he looked and he burned with hot anger and even hotter desire. There she was spread across the bed for his benefit, sin in miniature and only minimally clad in silk. And she looked shameless, sexy and stunning. It was a combination that did something quite disgraceful to his healthy libido.

Encountering the chillingly cool light in Antonio's stunning eyes, Sophie flushed to the roots of her hair and sat up with a jerk to hug her knees. She felt like an absolute idiot and almost cringed, for his disinterest was palpable. 'I was getting dressed…and I just decided to lie down for a nap,' she lied in a stricken surge, sliding off the bed in such clumsy haste that she almost fell.

'Did you know that Lydia wasn't my brother's child?' Antonio murmured smooth as silk, his tone conversational.

At that entirely unexpected question, Sophie froze like a fawn in flight and her green eyes opened very wide in response. 'Say that again…'

'If you are trying to convince me that you had no suspicion, you're wasting your time,' Antonio retorted with scornful bite. 'I can't believe you didn't know. How *could* you not have known? Your sister lived with you while she was pregnant and you were best friends—'

'Let me get this straight…out of the blue you are attempting to suggest that Lydia might *not* have been Pablo's kid?' Sophie recounted in strained interruption. 'What is this? Some sort of horrible bad joke?'

'If only,' Antonio riposted, lean, darkly handsome features hard as steel. 'I feel that you should be aware that you'll have to do more than prance round the bedroom in sexy knickers to dig yourself out of this particular tight corner!'

'How am I in a tight corner?' Sophie demanded, striving not to show any response to that mortifying reference to both her appearance and her behaviour. 'Just you explain why you're suddenly throwing all this rubbish at me. Have you any idea how insulting you're being?'

'Is there a polite way to put this? Belinda slept with

someone other than my brother and that man was Lydia's father.'

'Don't you dare try to smear my poor sister's reputation with disgusting lies!' Sophie shouted at him, her temper flaring as she stared at him in bewildered disbelief.

'It may be disgusting but it's not a lie. DNA tests have been carried out on me and on Lydia and I have the paperwork that assures me that there is no question of there being a blood relationship between us—'

'How could you have had DNA tests carried out?' Sophie gasped. 'That's not possible!'

'The tests were done a couple of weeks ago when I took Lydia to see Navarro Teruel—'

'You went behind my back and—'

'It wasn't like that—'

'It was exactly like that!' she flung fierily.

'I knew DNA testing would be necessary even before I came to England to see you. My lawyer warned me that the very fact that Lydia was born after Pablo and Belinda broke up and after his death might awaken doubts about the child's paternity. *Qué demonios!* It is most ironic that I had no doubts but those tests had to be done to protect the child in the future—'

Her head was reeling with the twists and turns of his explanation. 'I can't accept what you're saying. Why would people think such nasty things about an innocent child?'

'When there's money involved even my relatives are not above malicious conjecture.'

Sophie was more confused than ever. 'Money? What money?'

'My grandmother is a wealthy woman. The minute she learned of Lydia's existence she decided to alter her will and leave a substantial legacy to her great-granddaughter,' Antonio clarified coolly. 'For that reason even I saw the good sense of proving now by whatever means possible that Lydia was my brother's legitimate heir.'

'I had no idea about the legacy or your grandmother's plans,' Sophie admitted unevenly. 'But that doesn't excuse you taking advantage of me being ill to have tests done on Lydia that I didn't know about!'

'At the time my main goal was that she should have a full medical examination. I didn't want to worry you with my concern but she seemed very small and frail to me—'

'Thought I'd been neglecting her, did you?' Sophie stabbed jaggedly.

'No, my concern related to the fact that a couple of babies in this family were born with heart murmurs.'

'Right, OK,' Sophie groaned. 'But what is this gobbledegook about Lydia not being Pablo's child?'

'She *isn't* his child,' Antonio asserted grimly. 'DNA tests have proved that.'

'I still don't believe you…either you've picked this up wrong or you're lying for some weird reason of your own!' Sophie condemned wildly in her desperation. 'Belinda was married to Pablo and there was nobody else in her life until after Lydia was born. Somebody has made a dreadful mistake.'

Antonio dealt her a derisive look of distaste. 'You're wasting my time with these empty protests. It is my belief that you and Mrs Moore were well aware that Lydia was not related to me. I also think that you hoped to make money out of the deception—'

'What deception?' Sophie exclaimed so sharply that

her voice broke, for she was feeling increasingly out of her depth.

'I believe you expected me to pay you handsomely to look after the child in England. I'm a rich man. It was well worth your while to try and pass off Lydia as my brother's child—'

'That's the most revolting suggestion I've ever heard and you seem to be forgetting that my sister named you as one of her child's guardians in her will. Was she also in on this deception? Are you saying that my sister knew she was going to die?' Sophie asked him in disgust. 'And what on earth has Norah Moore got to do with all this?'

Antonio vented an embittered laugh. 'She was the ace up your sleeve. Things weren't looking too good for you that day that we talked on the beach, were they? I had every intention of taking Lydia back to Spain and you weren't going to make much profit out of that. So what did you do?'

Sophie jerked a thin shoulder. 'I don't know…you have this amazing imagination,' she breathed curtly, fighting her pain with all her might because it hurt so much that their relationship could disintegrate so fast into a welter of crazy accusations and suspicions. 'You tell me what I supposedly did next.'

'You sent Mrs Moore to see me at my hotel the next morning—'

Sophie fixed startled eyes on him. 'What the heck are you talking about?'

'And the woman made an excellent job of engaging my sympathies.'

'If Norah did come to see you, I knew nothing about it—'

'It was too neat the way it happened,' Antonio countered, unimpressed by her plea of innocence. 'Of course you knew about it. Your good friend, Norah, told me that I couldn't possibly separate you from Lydia because, having suffered childhood leukaemia, you were infertile. I swallowed the sad story and in common with most men I was reluctant to question you about that particular personal tragedy.'

Listening to him, Sophie felt as though she had been kicked in the teeth and betrayed. When he referred to her fertility problems, she turned as pale as milk. The terrible heavy silence lay while she fought to recover from that wounding blow and still hold her head high. 'I had no idea that Norah had sneaked off to see you to plead my case for me. She had no right to tell you my personal business,' she whispered sickly. 'And I'm sorry you were embarrassed like that, but I'd have drunk poison sooner than ask for your sympathy!'

Antonio could not drag his penetrating dark eyes from her heart-shaped face. She looked traumatised. He knew instantly that Norah Moore's visit to his hotel had not been a part of any scam and that what the older woman had told him in confidence about Sophie was true. Appalled at the manner in which he had confronted her on that sensitive issue, he was filled with immediate regret. His superb bone structure taut below his bronzed skin, he made an instinctive move towards her. 'Sophie…if that's true, I'll—'

'You'll what? Yes, it's true about the leukaemia and the infertility, but none of that has anything to do with this conspiracy theory you've dreamt up about Lydia,' Sophie spelt out, stepping back out of his reach and snatching up a wrap to dig her arms into the sleeves and cover her trembling body from view. 'I don't believe what you're saying, but I don't really care either.

Lydia is still Lydia and still my niece and she doesn't need a snobby uncle or a great grandmother's money… She never did need any of you when she already had me. And whatever happens she's *still* got me!'

Having completed that stricken assurance of intent and independence, Sophie vanished into the bathroom and slammed shut and locked the door. He knocked and she ignored it. He tried to reason with her through the door and she told him to shut up and leave her alone. He threatened to get the master key and use it unless she came out of her own volition and she told him she'd scream the place down and make such a fuss the staff would still be talking about it in a hundred years' time.

CHAPTER TEN

SOPHIE sat on the cold mosaic tiled floor and hugged her knees and stared into space.

It was all over. Her crazy romantic hopes, her living for today and not worrying about tomorrow, their marriage. All over. Suddenly Antonio was willing to believe that she was a lying cheat, a greedy, money-grabbing fraudster. She had had no idea just how fragile their understanding was. But now their relationship already seemed as imaginary and insubstantial as a child's soap bubble and she felt terrifyingly as if she were waking up in a living nightmare. In the space of minutes Antonio had taken her love and her pride and even her faith in him and destroyed the whole lot. As if it meant nothing, and obviously what they had shared *did* mean nothing to Antonio.

Sophie suppressed the sob clogging up her aching throat. How could she be so selfish that she was only thinking of her own predicament? What about Lydia? If Lydia was not a Rocha, she stood to lose so much: her new family, her home and her promising future. Nor could Antonio be expected to continue acting as a father-figure. About the only thing that Sophie knew about DNA tests was that they were reputed to be foolproof. Yet she still found it almost impossible to credit that the sister she had believed she knew so well could have been unfaithful to Pablo while they were still living together as a couple.

At the same time Sophie was reluctantly recalling

Norah Moore's crack about Belinda being a dark horse. The older woman had also suggested that Belinda had only ever told her kid sister what she reckoned she would want to hear. Sophie's heart sank as she ran those revealing comments back and forth inside her head. Obviously, Norah knew more than she had been prepared to admit about Belinda and Sophie would have to approach the older woman to see if she could cast some light on the situation.

But right now Antonio's anger was a painfully convincing body of proof and if he was right, Lydia was some other man's child. Antonio would not throw around such damaging allegations without strong evidence. He had been upset too, she acknowledged, her throat convulsing. He had become fond of Lydia. But it had been a mistake to forget that Antonio had only married her to give his supposed niece a mother and a stable home.

Sophie hugged her knees to her breasts. Norah had spilled her deepest secret to Antonio. Norah had told him she couldn't have a baby. She wanted to chase after him and tell him that her condition wasn't that cut and dried and final and that she just might have a tiny chance of conceiving. But what would be the point? Her face crumpled and she sucked in a quivering breath, fighting to keep control of her wildly see-sawing emotions.

She even understood why Norah had intervened and told Antonio. The older woman had been trying to help Sophie keep the baby she loved. Norah had quite deliberately treated Antonio to a sob story in a desperate attempt to shame and embarrass him into going away and leaving Sophie and Lydia alone. Of course, it had not occurred to Norah that Antonio's response to that sob story would be a marriage proposal. No wonder the older woman had been so dismayed at the prospect of Antonio marrying Sophie for Lydia's sake. For Norah had known that Antonio's most driving motivation could only have been pity.

The tears overflowed from Sophie's eyes in a hot, stinging flood, but not a sound escaped her, for she was determined not to let Antonio hear her cry. But what she had just been forced to accept was the most painful truth she had ever had to swallow. There it was, whether she liked it or not: Norah had pulled the right strings with Antonio. Antonio did loads for charity. Antonio was stuffed full of decent principles and conscience. And Antonio would have felt desperately sorry for Sophie when he realised that Lydia was likely to be the closest she ever got to a baby of her own. So, he had decided that he could not deprive her of Lydia and that was the only reason he had offered her marriage…the pity vote. She felt hollow with hurt and humiliation and the sheer agony of his rejection and the tears kept on falling for a long time.

Two hours later, Sophie emerged from the bathroom. She was very surprised to find Antonio still waiting. 'What do you want?' she asked, blanking him for it hurt far too much to let herself look directly at his darkly handsome features.

'When I got the news about Lydia, I lost my head…I'm sorry, *querida*,' Antonio breathed tautly. 'It was the shock but that is no excuse for the way I took my anger out on you.'

'Yeah, well, you won't be doing that again,' Sophie responded stonily from the dressing room where she was stuffing a change of underwear into a carrier bag.

'I won't be,' Antonio conceded. 'We will deal with this challenge together—'

Sophie rolled her eyes at her carrier bag. 'No, thanks. This isn't a challenge…trust you to call it something like that. This is the end of something that never should have begun.'

Antonio appeared in the doorway. 'What are you doing?'

'Packing a few things.'

His big, powerful body went rigid. 'Packing…to go where?'

'Back home.'

'This is your home.'

'No, this is *your* home. I want to speak to Norah and find out if she does know more about Belinda than I did. I assume the DNA tests you mentioned are correct and if it's at all possible I would like to know who Lydia's father is.'

'I'll come with you.'

Sophie compressed her soft pink mouth into a line tighter than a jar with a child-proof lid. 'No, this isn't your business any more.'

Antonio released his breath in a hiss. 'Please let me express my—'

'I'm really not interested in hearing you express anything. You married me 'cos you thought Lydia was your brother's kid. She's not his kid, so we can call it a day now—'

'There is much more between us than that,' Antonio argued. 'You're furious with me and you have every right to be—'

'OK, so push off and give me peace to pack—'

'It would be foolish to embark on a journey at this

time of night. We'll rise early and fly over to London tomorrow—'

'I'm not flying any place with you. I already told you…Lydia and I aren't your business any more—'

'You're my wife and I will not let our marriage break down over this,' Antonio asserted fiercely.

Sophie vented a thin little laugh. 'Marriage? What marriage? We never had a marriage! We've had a good laugh and lots of sex, but that's it!'

Antonio reached for her. She twisted away with sufficient violence to persuade him of the need to back off. Green eyes feverishly bright, she shot him a warning glance. 'Stay away from me!'

'If I could take back what I said, I would,' Antonio intoned in a roughened undertone. 'But the very fact that you never told me that you were infertile made me suspect that Norah Moore had told me lies!'

Sophie lost colour, for she had not thought of matters from that angle. Although she was reluctant to admit it, she could see how her silence on that thorny topic would have roused his suspicion that Norah had been shooting him a line. 'I didn't tell you because we didn't have a proper marriage,' she said in an effort to defend herself.

'What do you call a proper marriage?'

'One where the guy doesn't says things like, "For now, let's enjoy being married," like it's a casual affair!'

Dark colour demarcated the slashing line of Antonio's high cheekbones. 'You have a point. But I would still argue that our marriage was as real as any other. All the elements that needed to be there were there—'

'Yeah, *were*…past tense. We had a good time, but

let's quit while we're still speaking!' Sophie retorted with a brittle smile.

Antonio breathed in deep. 'I'm flying to England with you.'

'I don't care what you do as long as you leave Lydia and me alone,' she muttered tightly.

'Lydia won't be accompanying us.'

'Excuse me?' Sophie tossed him a disbelieving look.

'Lydia is staying here at the *castillo* until we return.'

'But I wasn't planning on returning!' Sophie exclaimed. 'I want to take her with me—'

'No. Lydia goes nowhere without my agreement and I will not give it,' Antonio delivered without hesitation. 'You're not in the right frame of mind to make an important decision about her future.'

Her hands clenched into hurting fists. 'What do you care? Lydia's nothing to you now—'

Dark golden eyes sought and held her accusing gaze. 'That's not true. I'm angry that I didn't know the truth. But I care as much about Lydia at this moment as I did when I woke up this morning.'

'Well, whoopee for you…you can visit us every six months.'

'Lydia is not travelling to England with us tomorrow,' Antonio spelt out grimly, brilliant eyes welded to the tight set of her delicate profile. 'Perhaps by then you might be ready to let me talk and say what I really want to say.'

Her soft mouth quivered and she turned her back on him. 'You've said enough for one day.'

'Sophie…' He touched her shoulder.

She shrugged him off. The silence pounded and thudded. Then the door closed on his departure and she wanted to scream and scream to exorcise the agony inside her. She hadn't wanted him to stay. But she could not bear him to leave her. But what was she supposed to say to a guy who had made a huge sacrifice for nothing? He hadn't wanted to give up his freedom and marry. But he had truly believed that he had a duty of care towards Lydia. Yielding to temptation on their wedding night had led to a relationship he would never have sought on his own behalf. So he had made the best of things in the short term.

That was the sort of guy Antonio was…always set on doing the right thing no matter how painful it might be. She loved him a lot, but she didn't want his pity. She felt so ashamed of her sister's behaviour as well. Belinda's will had got them into a disastrous marriage and unfortunately Lydia would suffer the most from the fallout. Sophie could not accept that Antonio could still genuinely care about Lydia now that he knew she wasn't his niece.

The following afternoon, the jet landed in London. After a night spent tossing and turning in misery, Sophie had slept for most of the flight. Antonio watched her the entire time she slept. He covered her up with a rug. He pushed a pillow under her flushed cheek. Without even speaking to him she was putting up signs as big as placards to keep him in touch with her mood. She had left off her wedding ring and even the watch he had given her. She was wearing a T-shirt and shabby jeans that he recalled from his first visit to the caravan site. It bothered him that she should have held onto those garments in spite of her wardrobe of new clothes and the wealth that surrounded her. He could see that he was being not so much airbrushed out of her scheme of things as annihilated as though he had never existed.

'You can stay in the car,' Sophie told him uncomfortably outside Norah Moore's little bungalow. 'If there's anything to find out, I promise that I'll share it with you.'

She had phoned Norah to tell her that she was visiting and she had also told the other woman about the results of the DNA test.

'Did you know Lydia wasn't Pablo's?' Sophie asked baldly as the older woman put on the kettle.

Norah gave her a reluctant nod of assent.

'Why didn't you tell me?' Sophie groaned.

'Belinda begged me not to and after she had passed away I saw no reason to upset you—'

'I can't believe that my sister talked to you and not to me!'

The older woman grimaced. 'She was your big sister and she wanted you to look up to her. She didn't exactly plan to tell me either.'

'It's OK…I'm grateful that she did talk to you because at least now I can find out the truth.'

'Well, I called in one evening and found Belinda drinking. I gave her a right telling-off about drinking with a baby on the way and she just laughed. You know how silly she could be. She asked me if I'd be shocked if she told me that the baby wasn't her husband's kid. She was gasping to spill the beans to somebody.'

'What did she tell you about Lydia's father?'

'That she'd been with a bunch of different men she picked up in bars and didn't have a blind clue which one was responsible.' As Sophie studied her in consternation Norah folded her lips. 'She went off the rails for a while. It happens. Her marriage was breaking up. Pablo was out all the time and having other women on the side and she decided to have some fun of her own.'

Sophie wrinkled her nose. 'What a mess…what an

awful mess. But if she knew right from the start that Lydia wasn't Pablo's why did she name Antonio as a guardian in her will?'

'I bet she only had that will done after Pablo had been killed. I think she was ashamed and wanted to forget what she'd done. She wanted to pretend the baby *was* her husband's. She certainly regretted telling me the truth and took against me because of it,' the older woman reminded Sophie wryly.

'I also know that you went to see Antonio at his hotel,' Sophie admitted. 'He told me about it.'

Norah pulled a face. 'That backfired on me,' she confided ruefully. 'I expected Antonio to let you keep Lydia here and maybe help you out with a bit of money. Instead he went and asked you to marry him.'

'Now I understand why you were so against our marriage.'

'But I didn't want to interfere. How was I to know what was for the best? Antonio meant well by Lydia and I didn't want to be the one who spoilt that for the kiddie.' Norah studied Sophie and raised a brow. 'I was about to ask how marriage is treating you, but I can see Antonio's right and tight with his cash. You're still wearing the same jeans you had before you left. Well, at least he'll not be getting into debt like that brother of his!'

Sophie went very red in the face and hastened to dissuade Norah from the conviction that Antonio was seriously mean with money. Norah informed her with some satisfaction that her son had started dating a neighbour's daughter and that the relationship was looking serious. Sophie walked slowly back out to the limousine.

'You don't have to tell me anything if you don't want

to,' Antonio drawled in a trying-to-be-ultra-sensitive tone.

'Belinda went with a load of different blokes and so we're never going to be able to find out who Lydia's father is,' Sophie responded, determined not to reveal just how affronted she was by her late sister's behaviour.

'I'm her father now,' Antonio murmured very quietly.

'Believe me, if Lydia was grown up enough to know that you're prone to taking pity on little children and cleaners, she'd pretty soon tell you not to bother yourself!'

'What if I was to tell you that I didn't take pity on the cleaner…that I actually wanted the cleaner for myself,' Antonio murmured softly.

Sophie blinked, reran that statement in her mind, examined it from all angles and shot him a furious glance of condemnation. 'I'd know you were just feeling guilty about what you said yesterday and I wouldn't believe you.'

The flight back to Spain seemed endless to her. An evening meal was served on board, but she had little appetite for it. When the limousine was ferrying them through the wooded countryside, she finally succumbed to the lure of watching Antonio. After all, there would be few if any such opportunities in her future, she reminded herself. Their marriage was finished. What reason did they have to be married now? She would pack and return to England with a cheery wave. The cheery wave, the show of happy indifference, was an essential. At least if she walked out with her head high, she would leave with her pride intact. Antonio, on the other hand, was looking very bleak. But then he had amazing tact and a real sense of occasion, she reflected. It would hardly be polite or considerate of him to sit there wreathed in smiles at the prospect of divorcing her and regaining his freedom.

She wondered how long it would take her to get over him. Just then she felt as if the entire world were covered by a big dark storm cloud that shut out all the light. Her past track record on getting over Antonio was not inspiring. Her attention lingered on his bold masculine profile, the springy blue-black darkness of his hair, his classic nose, the ebony sweep of his lashes and the wide, sensual curve of his mouth. Heat prickled low in her pelvis and she found herself wondering if she could tempt him into bed just one more time, and she was so mortified by that thought that she punished herself by looking out the window instead.

By the time the battlemented towers of the *castillo* appeared on the horizon, Sophie was strung up as high as a kite with nervous tension. Set against the backdrop of hills clad with dense green forest, Antonio's ancestral home looked glorious. Grand though the ancient fortress was, it had, without her even realising it, become home to her.

She worried at her full lower lip, keeping her eyes very wide to hold back the tears that were threatening her. She was remembering breakfasts on the ironwork balcony when Antonio had cut up fresh fruit for her and made her feel like a princess. She was remembering how he had driven her crazy when he was trying to teach her to drive. She was remembering how nervous she had been before that first dinner party and how he had teased her out of her worries and boosted her confidence by convincing her that she was much cleverer than she had ever thought she was.

In a silence that echoed and without even needing to discuss a preference, they both opted to go straight up to the nursery. Lydia was fast asleep in her cot, gloriously unaware of the revelations that had rocked the world of the adults selected to care for her.

'Will you visit her?' Sophie heard herself ask Antonio tightly as she walked back out of the room again. It was painful to bear the strained silence where once they would have been cheerfully engaged in talking about Lydia.

'Lydia's not going anywhere,' Antonio retorted, slowing his long stride to match her slower pace.

'You don't have the right to tell me that—'

'This is not about rights. Regardless of what happens between us, I intend to continue playing an active role in Lydia's life.'

'I wonder if you will.' Unhidden cynicism edged Sophie's curt response to that declaration.

'You will find that I keep my promises, *mi amada*. What I say I will do, I will do—'

'Oh, stop being so stuffy and superior!' Sophie lashed out at him, her desperate unhappiness finding a vent in temper.

Antonio swore under his breath, smouldering golden eyes clashing with her defiant scrutiny. 'Don't speak to me in that tone.'

'Why? What are you going to do about it?' Sophie snapped like a cat ready to scratch.

Antonio tugged her to him with one powerful hand and trapped her between the wall and his lithe, powerful body. 'What you like best?'

Her heart started pounding like a road drill, her breath parting her lips in short little spurts. Her pupils dilated, she stared up at him, every sensitive skin cell on fire for him, every nerve ending singing with sexual awareness. She wanted him instantly and desperately.

'No...' Antonio told her with seething derision. 'No talk...no sex!'

Her soft lips fell open. Hot pink flooded her creamy complexion. Shaken eyes veiling, she twisted under his arm and stalked away. 'I didn't want—'

'Don't you dare lie to me!' Antonio launched at her wrathfully.

Sophie was shattered that Antonio had raised his voice. She paled, mortification eating her alive. Just by looking at her he had realised she wanted him. How much else did he know? That she loved him?

'Antonio...'

'But even if you won't talk, you can at least listen,' Antonio delivered, lean, strong face grim and, with that assurance, he bent down and scooped her up into his arms.

'When you're in the middle of having an argument with someone, you don't just lift the person up in the middle of it and carry them away!' Sophie hissed enraged.

Antonio settled enquiring eyes on her furiously flushed face. 'Why not?'

'Because it's disrespectful...that's why!' Sophie declared.

Antonio shouldered open the bedroom door and, pausing only to kick it resoundingly shut behind him, he strode over to the bed and settled her firmly down on the edge of it.

'You want to talk? OK...I'll say it all for you,' Sophie told him jerkily.

'Why didn't I think of that? I really should take you into the office with me—'

'Look, I can't joke about this!' All of a sudden Sophie was finding it impossible to maintain her act of insouciance. 'But you know we only got married because you believed Lydia was your niece.'

'No, I don't know that,' Antonio responded infuriatingly.

Sophie fixed strained eyes on him, her heart-shaped face tight with tension and very pale. 'This is not the time to be smart. You thought you had to be a father to Lydia and you felt sorry for me because Norah had mentioned that I couldn't h-have k-kids...'

Antonio unfroze from his intimidating stance over her and hunkered down at the side of the bed so that their eyes were on a level. 'That's not important, *mi amada*.'

'Of course it's important...how can you say it's not?' Sophie gasped, the tears clogging her vocal cords making every word a challenge, her restive hands twisting together.

'It's sad,' Antonio murmured gruffly, and he unlinked her tense fingers with gentle pressure and held them in his. 'But you survived leukaemia and there was a price to pay. I am very grateful that you are alive and healthy today.'

'Why?' Sophie whispered shakily, in the dark as to where the dialogue was travelling.

Shimmering dark golden eyes captured her bemused gaze. 'I can do without having children but I don't think I could live without you.'

For a heartbeat Sophie was as still as a statue, for she could not accept that he could feel that way. She dragged in a shivering breath. 'You can't mean that...you can't. You're just feeling sorry for me—'

'I don't feel sorry for you. I was sad that you were infertile, but it's not that uncommon these days and there are various remedies like adoption. It's not the end of the world. I can see that it is still a great source of regret to you, but I have come to terms with it,' Antonio imparted intently.

'But how can you?' Sophie mumbled, scarcely knowing what he was telling her.

'People have adapted to far worse news. If our positions were reversed, if I was infertile, would you turn away from me?'

'No!' Sophie exclaimed instantly and then, colouring, added hastily, 'But that's different.'

'How is it different?'

'I don't have a title to pass on.'

'Titles such as mine are not of much use in today's world,' Antonio informed her levelly.

Sophie swallowed convulsively. 'There is a small chance that I might be able to conceive. The doctors don't really know how much damage was caused by the treatment I had when I was ill…but I wouldn't want you to get your hopes up.'

'I wouldn't. In fact I would suggest we don't even think of that slight possibility. Each of us has only one life and should make the most of it. I have found a happiness with you greater than anything I have ever known and I refuse to give that up,' Antonio swore, his keen gaze alight with fierce sincerity.

The silence lasted a long time while she tried to find fault with that far-reaching statement, for she was almost afraid to credit that he might mean it and afraid to believe that happiness might be within her reach after all.

'You refuse…you mean…are you saying you want to stay married to me even though I can't have kids?' Sophie almost whispered.

'Sí, enamorada,' Antonio confirmed.

Her green eyes were huge. 'I really make you that happy?'

'You do…'

'So you don't think a divorce would be a good idea?' she pressed unevenly.

'Not a question of it,' Antonio told her boldly and, springing fluidly upright, he drew her up with him. 'I couldn't let you go…ever. It's amazing. I never knew I could feel like this. I am head over heels in love with you.'

Her eyes shone and her whole face lit up. 'Seriously?'

Antonio tugged her to him with possessive hands. 'Very seriously. Lydia gave me the excuse to be with you and I grabbed it. My ability to make rational decisions went haywire the minute I saw you again. I even enjoyed fighting with you. Isn't that crazy? Nothing went according to plan—'

'Our wedding day was awful—'

'I wanted you to wear a long white dress,' Antonio confessed with an apologetic grimace. 'When you wore that flowery outfit, I thought you were making a joke of the occasion.'

'Oh, no, I wish I'd known that. I thought you'd be furious if I went for the full bridal show!' Sophie lamented.

'It's not your fault. I didn't know what I wanted until it was too late.' The regret in Antonio's steady dark golden eyes touched her heart. 'I didn't do any of the stuff I should've done to make the day special for you.'

'But you're brilliant at wedding nights,' Sophie hastened to tell him. 'That was special.'

'I didn't even realise how I felt about you. When you made that crack about picking me as a stud, I was…I couldn't see the joke. I was angry, offended…hurt,' he finally admitted grittily.

Sophie wrapped her arms tightly round him in apology. 'I was too busy worrying about how I could save face to see how you were feeling. When I don't feel sure of myself, I tend to go on the offensive.'

'I stayed away from you and I was incredibly miserable. I didn't recognise what was wrong with me until I came back and saw you again,' Antonio admitted, his fingers tilting up her chin so that he could scan her upturned face with appreciative eyes. 'I realised that I had a lot of work to do to try to turn our relationship round and make you happy.'

'You really succeeded at that…' Her throat tightened on the words for powerful emotions were coursing through her. 'You know, I have feelings for you too but I've been doing everything I could to hide the fact.'

'Like threatening to take Lydia and leave me?' Antonio gritted, but he was stroking gentle fingers across her cheekbone in a caress. 'Don't ever do that again. I messed up when it came to dealing with the DNA tests, but over the last twenty-four hours you almost ripped my heart out. I was so scared I was going to lose you and all over something that doesn't matter a damn.'

'You were shocked when you found out that Lydia wasn't your niece— I'm not blaming you for thinking the worst of me as well. You didn't think that way for long,' she pointed out forgivingly. 'But how can you say that Lydia's parentage doesn't matter?'

'Being Pablo's daughter would always have been something of a poisoned chalice for her. People have long memories and my brother had a bad name,'

Antonio remarked ruefully. 'At least Lydia won't suffer that stigma.'

Sophie was grateful that he was all for an open and honest approach to Lydia's background. 'You'll have to tell Doña Ernesta. Will she be very upset?'

'My grandmother will be disappointed, but she'll cope. I think we should adopt Lydia.'

'Oh, could we? I'd love to do that.'

'I don't think Belinda planned to lie about Lydia,' Antonio said then. 'After my brother's death, I tried several times to persuade her to let me visit and she always put me off. She must've been pregnant then and at that point she evidently wasn't thinking of passing off her baby as Pablo's.'

'That must've come later, probably because she wanted to forget that she'd gone a little wild.'

'Lydia's beautiful. Let's be glad she's ours,' Antonio suggested.

Her smile was as bright as the sun. 'That's how I always feel about her.'

'Would you now like to tell me about those feelings that you said you were determined to hide from me?' Antonio prompted tautly.

Sophie went pink when she realised that she still hadn't told him she loved him. 'I love you…lots and lots and lots.'

Golden eyes ablaze with satisfaction, Antonio snatched her off her feet and kissed her with all the fire of his passionate temperament. One kiss led to another and matters became pretty heated very quickly. A long time afterwards, while they lay secure in each other's arms, Antonio tried to get her to promise that she would rerun the 'fancy lingerie and supper on the floor' seduction routine for his benefit again. She said she'd have to think about that very carefully, while secretly planning to indulge him on his birthday.

Just over a year later, when Lydia's adoption was finalised, Sophie and Antonio threw a massive party at the *castillo* to celebrate the occasion.

Sophie felt a little out of sorts that evening and over the next month she suffered several other minor but irritating symptoms. When she consulted Dr Teruel, she discovered that she was three months pregnant. Her joy and Antonio's knew no bounds. They shared every tiny milestone of the pregnancy with intense interest and gratitude.

Their daughter, Carisa, was born without complications. Lydia was so excited about having a little sister that she brought all her toys to Carisa and was disappointed to learn that it would be some time before the baby could play with her. Doña Ernesta comforted Lydia with the suggestion that she would be able to teach Carisa all her favourite games and tell her stories.

Sophie's grasp of Spanish was by then fluent and she began attending a part-time course on textile conservation. Lydia was almost five years old when Sophie conceived for a second time. Sophie gave birth a month early to two little boys, who quickly gained weight and made up for their premature arrival in the world. They called the twins Francisco and Jacobo. Their christening was celebrated at the Rocha home in Madrid. A very flattering set of photos and a brief interview would later appear in an up-market magazine in return for a sizeable charitable donation. Antonio had come to accept that his wife was something of a celebrity and her public liked to see her in print.

'I have a surprise, *enamorada*,' Antonio confided the

night of the christening when all the children were finally tucked up and asleep and even the most long-staying guest had gone home. He made her close her eyes as he slid a ring on her finger, but it stuck on her knuckle and she had to push a little and peep.

'Oh, my goodness!' she gasped then, impressed to death by the starry sparkle of the huge diamond. 'What's this for?'

'It's your engagement ring…just a few years late,' Antonio teased tenderly. 'Would you still say yes if I asked you to marry me?'

Sophie gave him a huge smile, happiness bubbling through her. 'Yes, I'm still crazy about you.'

Antonio closed her into his arms and met her warm green eyes. 'I will never stop loving you,' he promised her and she believed him, all her former insecurity long since cured by his love and care.